A Thousand Eyes

A Thousand Eyes

Junior Burke

Winchester, UK
Washington, USA

First published by Cosmic Egg Books, 2018
Cosmic Egg Books is an imprint of John Hunt Publishing Ltd., Laurel House, Station Approach,
Alresford, Hants, SO24 9JH, UK
office1@jhpbooks.net
www.johnhuntpublishing.com

For distributor details and how to order please visit the 'Ordering' section on our website.

Text copyright: Junior Burke 2017

ISBN: 978 1 78535 715 2
978 1 78535 716 9 (ebook)
Library of Congress Control Number: 2017937407

A CIP catalogue record for this book is available from the British Library.

Design: Stuart Davies

Printed and bound by CPI Group (UK) Ltd, Croydon, CR0 4YY, UK

We operate a distinctive and ethical publishing philosophy in
all areas of our business, from our global network of authors to
production and worldwide distribution.

For Michele and Simone, and also for Bodhi

"The night has a thousand eyes, and the day but one;
Yet the light of the bright world dies, with the dying sun."
Francis W. Bourdillon

PART ONE

RUSTLINGS

CHAPTER 1

He did his killing at night. One time he waited too long and had to strike in the harsh, gray light but he would not wait that long again. His hunger was too deep, his thirst too strong.

Moving along the river now, branches and leaves were brushing his face and sides; the damp ground beneath him, the rushing current just beyond. Nothing stirring. Nothing worth taking, anyway. The river swerved toward him and he bounded into it, feeling the wetness as he splashed, pushing off a flat rock, clearing the remaining water in one leap.

He cleared the rise, then was on smooth, hard ground, a sensation he did not like. In the open now, he did not sense he was being seen. Still he moved swiftly until he reached the place where the lights often came right at him, although there were none at the moment. Speeding up, he passed beyond where he felt exposed. He did not like being seen, not by anything – watching and waiting, striking when there was no chance for his victim, who would surrender the throat, the flank, all the rest. He would have his way, then cover his kill with branches and leaves so he could come back and finish. He would usually return more than once.

Now, like the river, the smooth, hard ground bent to the right. Ahead, were places he would go to only when there was little choice.

As he neared the spot where clouds often poured out thick and pale from above, he halted. The clouds had disturbed him, but never like this. There was a funnel, a tower of ash and blackness, pushing upwards to the dark blue sky, a blinding flame licking the center, crimson and orange shooting in all directions. His nose, eyes and tongue were under attack in a way he had never experienced. A cry rose within him, swirled in his throat, causing a whimper he could not recognize as his own.

His instincts told him to go no further, to retreat back to the mountains. He was desperate and hungry but something had come to the valley more lethal than even he was, putting every living thing at risk.

Back on the hard ground now, lights were training on him from beyond. His eyes stung from what he had encountered. Bright and glaring, the lights got even brighter, came even closer. He moved faster, toward the tree line on the other side, dense brush beyond it. Tonight he would need to settle for a small kill, a coon or a rabbit, not the deer or elk he had been seeking.

Although a loner, with the smell and smoke and taste still harsh in his nostrils, eyes and throat, he needed to warn others, not just his own kind but all other non-humans.

Death was in the air.

* * *

Lynton, Colorado was a town caught between two eras. One part of it, the older, classic, part consisted of those whose names and roots had been in town for a few generations or more. Others had moved there around the turn of the most current century, many of them from Boulder; those who no longer wanted or could afford to be in a housing market that was among the steepest in the nation. The rest of the more recent arrivals were from other parts of the country, who'd come to Colorado for the air and the mountains and decided to try small town life with access to Boulder's rarified sensibilities and Denver's international airport.

In Lynton, these were not geographical separations. The storied locals lived among the fresher, shinier newcomers and on the surface it all seemed to blend. So there was diversity but not in the way that word has come to be used. Lynton, like the majority of Colorado, was white and spoke English. Those who claimed Spanish as a first language might work at the Mentex cement plant, Lynton's only substantial industry, but when their shift was concluded they would head home to Valmont, seven miles out on the plains. With a population of two thousand, Lynton remained a small town, but around and above it, more and more newer and bigger houses were dotting the hills and pushing out the borders.

The mountains provided a huge natural wall to the west, like a massive mural, imposing and mysterious. You could drive or bike or walk up into them but they were an increasingly small part of the world that had not been disturbed and was not to be underestimated. They were also home to a range of species who, in any unforeseen encounter, might not surrender in the face of what most humans thought of as civilization.

There was only one church in Lynton, the First Methodist. The Catholics used it for Saturday evening Mass and a non-denominational meditation group rented it on Thursday nights. All others were forced to worship in neighboring towns. If you wanted a church wedding in Lynton, First Methodist was where you had it, and for a funeral service, it was also the site. For Frank Kincaid's funeral, the church was swelled to its two-hundred capacity.

Frank, who had worked at the Mentex plant for nearly ten years, was well-known in town and widely respected for his role with the volunteer fire department. His wife Ginger was bravely addressing those assembled, but barely holding up. She was pale, eyes stunned behind oval, silver-rimmed glasses, her light-shaded hair of no discernible color. In this grief-filled moment she projected a kind of noble beauty.

"Frank loved this community and loved this part of the world. He'd fish in the summer and hunt elk with his bow in the winter, so we would have fresh trout on the grill and fresh meat in the freezer..." She looked down tearfully at her young daughters, April and Kara. "We all remember the Gold Canyon fire, three years back. That was a Labor Day weekend and Frank's brother

4

was coming in from Nebraska." Ginger nodded at Kent in the second row, back straight, smiling through tears. "Once that fire started sweeping, Frank was out there day and night. I think Kent got to see him only once in seventy-two hours."

Kent, seated on the aisle, nodded in affirmation.

Ginger continued. "A number of homes were lost in the valley, but even when the winds shifted, Frank and the other fighters were able to keep the flames from spreading to town. That night, he was as tired as I'd ever seen him. As he was lying next to me, he said, "Maybe I haven't done much in my life that will be remembered, but you know what, Gin? This weekend, I helped put out a fire...""

During the post-service gathering in the church's community room, Ginger was receiving a line of mourners that stretched from the hall, putting what she had left into greeting and being greeted. Her girls were doing their parts, talking in low tones and listening solemnly, as their dad would have expected of them.

A trim, fortyish woman whose black hair was styled very short took hold of Ginger's hand. "My name's Angie Prez. You don't know me, Ginger, and Frank didn't know me either. But you and I need to talk."

CHAPTER 2

Lowell Felker, manager of Mentex Colorado, and Ned Haddock mayor of Lynton, were facing each other on opposite sides of Lowell's glass-top desk in his fourth floor office. The mayor had on a dark suit and tie, Lowell, a sports coat, slacks and cowboy boots. At fifty-three Lowell was five years older than Haddock and at six-three, a half-foot taller. He was broader too, big shouldered, his complexion ruddy and weathered, in contrast to the mayor's pallid skin. The mayor's hair was thinning, unlike Lowell's which was thick and yellowish-white, being between dye-jobs. Lowell's eyebrows were also thick, above eyes that were small in contrast to everything else about him and, at the moment, those eyes appeared agitated. There was an open fifth of Maker's Mark on the desk and Lowell was pouring a fresh glass for himself while Haddock's full glass stood all but untouched on the desk.

"I don't understand you, Ned. Why would you let something like this get in the way of your making a fortune?"

"Something like a man losing his life? Did you see his kids at the funeral?"

Lowell took a gulp of bourbon. "Frank left here and keeled over in his own house. Hell, for all anyone knows, his heart was a time bomb waiting to happen."

"You and your crew screwed up, Lowell. And Kincaid put himself in charge of the clean-up and got his lungs full of poison."

"He knew the risks, was just as greedy as the rest of us."

Haddock stood up. "I'm sure you'll find a way of going ahead with your project, but I'm pulling out."

Lowell pushed his chair back. "Why the hell would you do a dumb-ass thing like that?"

"I don't care how much money anybody stands to make. I don't want any part of this anymore." He looked around as though there might be something he'd brought along that he needed to take with him.

Now Lowell stood. "What about the rezoning?"

"Get somebody else to do it."

Lowell laughed but there was no mirth in it. "Who else is gonna get it done for us, Ned? You're the mayor for Goddsakes."

Haddock looked at Lowell. "That's something you're going to have to figure out on your own, my friend."

"You're a damn fool, Haddock, turning up your nose at the opportunity of a lifetime. And you might think you're washing your hands of this but the kind of dirty your hands have gotten doesn't wash off so easily."

Ned didn't reply on his way out the door.

He crossed the hall to the elevator, took it down, then crossed the lobby and stepped out into the dusk. He pulled out a cigarette. He'd started smoking again when this whole business with Lowell Felker had started and now, as he lit up and inhaled deeply, he vowed that this would be his last smoke. It would be such a relief to get away from Felker and from this venture of his that seemed doomed the deeper Ned involved himself. Felker would have to find someone else to sell out the town.

As he stood there, Ned glanced toward the brush that bordered the parking lot. He felt he'd caught a glimpse of something, some subtle motion, but as his eyes probed the trees and branches he couldn't make out anything unusual. He took a last pull on the cigarette, then dropped it on the pavement and pressed it lifeless with the sole of his shoe. He unlocked his Audi wagon, pulled open the door and climbed behind the wheel.

It only took a minute to reach the stoplight at the entrance to town, and it was green for a change. It would take another full minute to come upon any concentrated real estate, Lynton's borders were larger than needed to accommodate such a small community.

Highway 64 turned into North Center Street, which ran one

way through town and pointed toward the mountains. Once he'd cleared the two main blocks of Lynton, Ned was on Highway 38, winding steadily upward.

After two miles, he turned right on Sandyhill Road, which led to his place. He wondered if Kyle and Jessica would be there. No, Kyle said they were driving in to Boulder to meet some old high school friends for dinner. Kyle was home from his junior year at Northwestern and Jessica was his fiancée, wedding plans for as soon as they graduated next June. Ned's wife, Susan had left for Pennsylvania at the news that her father had been moved to a hospice, so she hadn't seen Kyle yet or met her prospective daughter-in-law. Before going, Susan informed Ned that Jessica's mother made a point of mentioning on the phone that Jessica and Kyle had not shared a bedroom when they'd visited Jessica's home in Indiana the week before.

"You think they're not sleeping together at college, Susan?" Ned had replied.

"Of course they are. But the woman feels strongly about it. I don't want to start any trouble. Just put her downstairs in the guest room, and she and Kyle can work it out."

Ned parked in the drive and made his way to the door. He loved his house. Some visitors, he assumed, found it cold, with its cement walls and floors. But there were vast windows that looked through the trees and out on the mountains to the west and north, the valley to the east and south. At night, the twinkling lights of Lynton, the town he and Susan had embraced ten years before, after moving from Palo Alto, would smile up at them.

He'd enjoyed being mayor, had given it his best for seven years, until that damn Felker roped him into his scheme. Ned had been dazzled by the prospect of quick and lasting money, even though it went against most of what he'd come to believe. And, damn it, Felker was right, Ned would need to keep his mouth shut because, as Felker so impudently pointed out, Ned Haddock's hands had gotten dirty.

* * *

Ned was in his bed asleep when he was awakened by noise from downstairs. Kyle was making a racket, banging things around in the kitchen. What time was it? Ned turned and looked at the glowing numbers from the clock on the bedside table. Three-thirty-two. Rattle, rattle. Crash. What the hell was Kyle up to down there?

Ned rose and flung on his bathrobe. He thought about turning on the lamp, then instead crossed the room, pulled the half-open door toward him and stepped out into the hall. Something caught his eye and Ned turned to the left. There was light coming from Kyle's room across the hall and Kyle was standing in the doorway in underwear and t-shirt, a look of consternation on his face. "Somebody's in the kitchen," he whispered.

Fighting through his freshly awakened state, Ned's mind began to spin. Susan wouldn't have flown home early, she would have called. He remembered his cell phone was on the bedside table. "I'll call nine-one-one," he whispered.

"Jessica's down there," uttered Kyle.

"Are you sure that isn't her?"

Another crash assailed their ears.

"Of course that isn't her. I'm going down."

"No, wait here. I'll make the call."

Ned went back into his room and turned on the bedside lamp. The phone was on the small table, plugged into an outlet. He fervently hoped he had service. Sometimes the altitude affected it. As he lifted the phone, he heard a cry, clearly Jessica's voice. "Kyle, what going on?"

Ned pressed the digits. Static, then nothing. From downstairs, he heard other sounds and then Kyle, shouting, "Hey, get out of here – get the hell out!" Followed by some kind of frantic thrashing.

Ned dropped the phone, crossed the bedroom and descended

the stairs. Near the bottom, he halted where he had a sight line into the kitchen. The refrigerator door was fully open and the light from it cast an eerie glow. Kyle was stretched out on the floor, a huge black form covering his body, looking like it was smothering him. Kyle's legs were quivering. A cry rose from somewhere inside Ned and the black form turned.

A bear, a huge one, rose on its hind legs, emitting a deep moan.

Ned gaped at the enormous creature. Blood was covering its snout, and what had been half of Kyle's neck dangled from its mouth.

Ned, frozen, tried to think of what he could get hold of, a carving knife from the drawer, anything. Then the bear, in a black mass of furious energy, was bounding up the stairs.

Ned flailed his arms but the bear's massive head butted his chest and Ned was sent upwards and back as though blasted by some tremendous explosion. Next thing he knew, he was on the floor in front of his bedroom as the five hundred pound bear once again rose to its full height of nearly six feet and let out a roar that shook the walls of the house.

The beast was on him again and Ned felt its exposed claws rake his face before it flung him toward the half-open door of the bathroom.

There was silence for a moment as Ned felt something in his eyes and realized it was his own blood. Then he was brutally picked up and thrown through the glass doors of the shower.

Ned lay in the tight space, dazed and grievously wounded. He curled up in a ball but the bear wasn't stopping. With raging teeth it ripped a huge piece of Ned's cheek then gnawed the top of his head, ripping the scalp open. Ned's blood was flowing as though a spigot had been turned on. He remained curled up in surrender with the bear bent over him, thrashing and tearing as though Ned Haddock were the last meal he would ever have.

* * *

Jessica Rafferty lay petrified, covers up to her chin, in an unfamiliar bed in an unfamiliar house. Whatever had happened in the kitchen was still happening upstairs.

She'd been awakened from a dream. In the dream, a tall man in a black hat and long black coat was trying to get in through the front door of Kyle's parents' house. Jessica had both hands tightly gripped on the doorknob and the intruder was on the other side. The man was pure evil. Jessica knew if she let him in he would try desperately to kill everyone in the house.

She'd woken up shaking with fear. Just when she heaved that 'only a dream' sigh of relief, she heard scratching, banging, things being tossed around. Had Mr. Haddock come home drunk? No, Kyle told her when they got home he was asleep upstairs. Why hadn't she and Kyle stayed in Boulder and gotten a hotel room as she'd suggested? Kyle's father wouldn't care, it was just Jessica's mother who always wanted to impose her own rules onto everything. Jessica hadn't been able to determine what was going on in the kitchen but whoever it was either thought nobody was home or just didn't care. For Jessica, the only way out of the house was to rush into the hallway and run to the front door, passing the open kitchen on her right. Whoever was in there might hear or see her. When she couldn't stand it anymore, she'd called out for Kyle.

Through it all, Jessica hadn't left the bed; it seemed like some kind of sanctuary for her. Nor did she get up when she heard Kyle rush down the stairs and shout at someone. Then came more and different sounds which, although closer and louder, had been very much like the ones she was hearing now from upstairs. It sounded like animal noises mixed with what seemed to be Mr. Haddock groaning in helpless agony.

This might be her only chance.

Jessica forced herself to sit up. She swung her legs and felt her feet on the floor. Dressed only in her sheer, mint-shaded nightgown, she yanked open the door, swung left and sprinted down the hall.

Flashing past the kitchen, out of the corner of her eye, she passed Kyle's t-shirt clad body on the floor. Her right foot went out from under her and she tumbled, the side of her head slamming against the wall. In the darkness and confusion, Jessica realized she'd just slipped on blood that had oozed out of Kyle's body and into the hallway.

Jessica shot back up, lurched to the front door and yanked it open. She lunged across the porch and darted down the steps.

As she swerved right, down the driveway, she could feel the night around her, the warm air filling her lungs as though providing a first breath. Jessica knew she would just keep running and wouldn't stop until she reached someplace safe.

Approaching the bottom of the driveway, she spotted something, a shape darker than the night. She swung to the right but it moved sideways with astounding fluidity. Jessica thudded into the solid black shape, then felt its strange and foreign power wrap around her. It raked her back and shoulders as its foul breath roamed her face. The beast butted with its head then clamped its teeth between her chin and lower lip. As Jessica's body collapsed, she still didn't know exactly what was on top of her, brutally batting both sides of her skull and devouring what had once been her smooth and beautiful face.

CHAPTER 3

It was nearly dawn and Officer Cinda Rigg was taking a last cruise around Juniper Park. She worked the overnight shift three times a week. Besides general cop duties, Cinda was the Lynton township officer in charge of animal control. At night, the ones she came across tended to be healthy. Calls during the day usually meant rabies or wasting disease. For the most part, she loved her job. That's why she was so grateful that Randall had covered for her two months before when she'd slipped. She'd stashed the pint under the seat of the township's Ford Explorer and Randall had found it. But he didn't turn her in, even gave it back to her. Cinda had poured the vodka down the sink as soon as she got home and began going to meetings. Still, it was all she could do during her night-time circuits to keep herself from pulling up to the window of Red Leaf Liquors, or popping into Sasquatch Wine and Spirits.

No! She didn't need a drink, she needed a meeting. There was one in the morning in the basement of the Methodist Church, she'd go to that. It was two hours after her shift was over at seven, giving her time to go home and make Ry breakfast and get him out the door for the bus to Y Camp. "Hello, my name's Cinda and I'm an alcoholic," she would tell them.

"Hello, Cinda," they would chime.

Sometimes the repetitive nature of the whole enterprise was numbing, but if you worked the program, it worked for you.

Cinda was from Auckland, New Zealand, had come to the States twelve years before and met Gordon in Denver, where her sister was living at the time. He followed up with e-mails, asking Cinda to come see him. That visit led to her pregnancy, a rushed marriage, a beloved son, and a welcomed divorce. Gordon lived in Boulder and the divorce decree stated that neither he nor Cinda could move from Colorado until Ry turned eighteen. That was seven years away. Cinda's life had taken turns she never would have anticipated and being a cop was one of them. She'd only had to draw her gun once, on Daniel Stoppard, who managed the local hardware store and was losing it during an argument with his estranged wife and her much younger boyfriend. But Stoppard had come to what senses he had, and put the knife down.

Her phone chimed and Cinda lifted it toward her. It was from the station. "Randall?"

"Yep. "I'm on my way in, should be there in five minutes."

"You need to go to one-thirteen Sandyhill Road. Some campers up there called in a possible homicide. The county wouldn't give away much on the phone. Whatever it is, it sounds like something they're not used to dealing with."

Homicide? The last one in Lynton had been six years ago, before Cinda joined the force, some family dispute over money. So this was going to push her shift into overtime. She thought about calling Norma, the woman who stayed with Ry at Cinda's home but then decided to just get up there and let Norma determine that something unusual had come up.

Cinda pushed it, siren wailing. Turning right, off the highway, she wove upwards. There was a guardrail to the right but it was challenging driving and Cinda reminded herself that even when the weather was dry like this, it was not unheard of for drivers to lose control on the steep incline.

A couple of miles in, Cinda rounded a curve and applied the brakes. There was a state patrol car and a county van, as well as a civilian car with a man and a woman sitting inside it. Cinda eased her Ford Explorer to the side and got out. Two Boulder County cops, one male, one female were standing off to the side.

"What've we got?" asked Cinda.

"That couple over there came across a body part on the side of the road," said the male cop. "There's a female corpse at the top of the driveway and she's missing an arm. Two other victims inside the house. The state's in there securing the scene. Before long it's going to get pretty crowded up here."

"The ones inside, are they still alive?"

"Two males, both dead."

Cinda walked up the driveway bracing herself for what she was about to see. She took a gulp of air, realizing she'd been to this house before, a town Christmas party a couple of years back. This was where the mayor, Ned Haddock, lived.

Although she was walking purposefully she froze, then involuntarily took a step back at the sight of a young woman lying on her back in a shredded nightgown, her face and chest ravaged. The eye that was still in its socket was trained on the sky as though she'd been praying or trying to comprehend what had just happened.

Cinda felt something rising up in her and she stepped across the driveway toward a slope that led down from the side of the house. Below was a small clearing and Cinda knew that if this feeling kept rising she would need to step down there and get rid of the revulsion swirling up within her.

And then she caught sight of something, a small, dark mound in the pristine grass. She stepped down and looked... Bear-scat, she'd seen it hundreds of times. This particular mass was comprised mostly of vegetation, purplish sarsaparilla seeds and several blueberries that had been swallowed whole. But something else caused Cinda to feel a fresh wave of nausea from even deeper in her gut.

Atop everything was a glowing diamond, set on a gold band, encircling what had once been a woman's finger.

CHAPTER 4

Todd Wendt pulled up to the gate of the high, chain-link fence that surrounded the Mexico City headquarters of Mentex International. An armed guard greeted him with small talk Spanish through the driver's side open window and Todd replied fluently. He was expected, vouched for. He guided his company-leased, red, Volkswagen Passat to a guest spot in the executive lot, then strode toward the towering, bronze-shaded structure. Todd was thirty-six, tanned and dark-haired, his linen suit a perfect fit. He moved with the confidence and assurance he needed to project for this occasion. Herman Sandoval, Chief Executive Officer, lorded from the twenty-seventh floor, and that's who Todd was there to see.

Received with well-practiced grace by the elegant female receptionist, Todd was offered water or a soft drink. He declined, then was introduced to Sandoval's assistant, also elegant and also female, and smoothly ushered into an office the size of a handball court.

Sandoval stood, all five-six, two-hundred-forty pounds of him, snugly fitted into a silk suit. His finely groomed hair was equal parts silver and black. He gestured toward a chair, rings and Rolex gleaming. "We have not formally met, Mr. Wendt, is that correct?" he said in subtly accented English, then eased back into his expansive armchair. Todd had reviewed scores of the man's on-camera presentations and briefings and knew him to speak with the formality of one who was foreign-born, yet educated at top American universities: in Sandoval's case, Georgetown and Harvard.

"Right, sir, this is the first time."

"I understand you have requested transfer."

Todd had heard that the man wasn't much for pleasantries. "Yes, sir. I put in for it at the beginning of the year."

"You are not displeased with the company, I hope?"

"Of course not, sir. Just homesick, really. Plus, we have so many U.S. plants, I'm hoping now that I'm in the flow of things, I could relocate to one of them."

Sandoval produced an expression that was difficult to read. "I started you here so you could learn the company from the inside out. From the evaluations and reports I've seen, it does seem you are ready to move toward permanent placement into one of our facilities as a vital part of its operation." There was a freshly cut corona on the gleaming desk in front of him, and Sandoval glanced down like he was about to reach for it, then decided not to. "We have a plant in Lynton, Colorado. A tiny town, but one of our most lucrative operations."

Todd's face clouded involuntarily. "I'm certainly aware of it."

"We have, in the past, encountered there what I would characterize as a bad press and things are flaring up again. It used to be we could address such trouble locally, but with the Internet..." He offered a gesture of futility, indicating what little control even a man of his stature had in the face of twenty-first century discourse. "There's been a troubling amount of online chatter. The plant manager, Lowell Felker, claims he has everything under control. Nonetheless, I would like you to go there to ensure that we continue to operate without undue disturbance."

"What's the source of the friction?"

"Lynton is a peculiar community. It is one part Old West cowboy town, but there is also a strident faction in and around it, rabidly opposed to our industry and its necessary practices. They used to apply non-stop pressure, but Felker has thankfully been able to keep such murmurings contained since he got there seven years ago. Still, we do not want to find ourselves again under a microscope, facing a fresh onslaught of EPA violations and sanctions."

Now Todd voiced what was troubling him. "Respectfully, sir,

I was hoping to be assigned somewhere... well, more populous and less remote."

Sandoval leveled his gaze at Todd. "You will not be in Lynton more than six months. That should provide ample time for you to assess what needs to be done in order to stay the course. Once that is accomplished, I will assign you anywhere you wish in the United States."

CHAPTER 5

At her desk in the police substation, getting ready for her night shift, two things were troubling officer Cinda Rigg. One was the state report she'd just filled out regarding the bear attack that killed Ned Haddock, his son Kyle and Jessica Lynn Rafferty. *What had actually happened that terrible night?* The bear had entered, undoubtedly looking for food. It raided the refrigerator, evidenced from the food strewn everywhere. Young Kyle had clearly come upon or confronted the animal and had been set upon in the kitchen. Then the bear went upstairs and attacked Ned Haddock. *But what about the rest of it?*

Jessica had been in the downstairs guest room; the bed had been slept in and strands of her hair were on the pillowcase. But the bear killed her outside. *How had that happened? Did it chase her out, then return to the house?* There were no signs of that. Bear tracks, complete with blood from both the Haddock men left the house as the animal made its way to a wooded area that sloped downward, west. Tracks appeared on the incline that led up from the opposite side of the driveway, so Cinda determined that was how the bear made its way to the house. Maybe the young woman heard noises and went out to investigate. That didn't make sense. Jessica Rafferty was in an unfamiliar setting, why would she put herself at risk? The whole horrible thing made no sense.

* * *

Wolfpaw would put on his deerskin moccasins and droopy hat, set out from his trailer on the edge of town, and walk through the night. He was getting older and needed to keep his senses keen. He would try to make sure that every living thing out there would be perceived by him first. Of course, he wasn't always successful; those non-human creatures were sharply-tuned. With some, he even shared secret communications, would send messages out to them and receive messages as well. Most times theirs were blurred, just shadows of caution or distress. And while most people in town regarded him as an unsettling presence – tall, scrawny, drooping mustache – he felt the creatures knew him as, if not a friend, then the only human who tried to understand them.

While his usual nightly excursions were general in purpose, tonight he was venturing out with something specific in mind. The mauling and murder of three people in a private home, one of them the mayor, was taken by the citizens of Lynton as a random tragedy. But Wolfpaw suspected otherwise. Ever since the accident at the Mentex plant, the creature population was unsettled in a way he'd never known. They at first avoided him, not calling out or acknowledging him as they did before, as though he'd been part of something shameful and they no longer felt they could trust him. They'd seemed frightened then turned angry. Breeds usually hostile toward each other were somehow in communication. Wolfpaw had seen an owl perched beside a golden eagle: a bobcat lying next to a fox.

He crossed the main road, then the small city park across from the post office. There, on the side street, the police van was easing toward him. That lady officer, the one with the English-type accent, was at the wheel, making her rounds. Her window came down as she pulled up beside him. "Aye, Wolfpaw, you come across any deer tonight?"

"Not seen a one."

"We've had some reports of wasting disease. The ones that got it will just come into somebody's yard and stay there. Poor things don't know what to do with themselves. You doin' okay tonight?"

"Doin' fine."

"Terrible, what happened up on Sandyhill Road."

Wolfpaw didn't feel like talking tonight. "Their world as much as ours."

"But three people? A bear doesn't usually go mad like that."

"Not until it does, lady officer."

To Cinda, Wolfpaw was usually friendlier. Tonight he seemed almost angry. "Take care now," she said, then pulled away.

Wolfpaw kept walking until he was out in the open, away from town, the mountains behind him, the plains ahead; sprawling fields on either side. The sky was violet-blue, the clouds silver-white, with a nearly full pearl of a moon.

The way he saw it, the bear attack had been not a culmination of the creatures' anger but a beginning and he wanted to make sure they were willing to take a course of action that would not harm innocent people. If they'd gone after the mayor, thinking he was behind the disturbance at Mentex, they'd already killed two others who likely had nothing to do with it.

All of it made Wolfpaw extremely restless and uneasy. He'd been wrestling with his emotions, fighting the urge to walk, not merely beyond town, but east, back to North Dakota, where he'd come from in the first place. His father had been of the Ottawa People and his mother, a second generation Norwegian. Wolfpaw returned home after his army discharge, then left on his twenty-first birthday, intending to hitch-hike all the way to the Pacific Northwest. But once he got to Colorado, everything he'd ever be looking for was here. He couldn't believe that more than an entire generation had passed since then. His father's parting words the day Wolfpaw walked out the door haunted him. "If you leave here walking, one day, you'll will return walking."

Wolfpaw wondered if that day had come. He felt like one from long before who, upon placing his ear against the ground, determined that a warring tribe was approaching, thundering ever closer.

He'd come out here, to the open fields, hoping to be directly contacted by the red-tailed hawk. She'd come to him on two previous occasions, once about the Gold Hill fire, and once about Mentex, even before the greedy fools started sending whatever new poison they were mixing into the sky. Walking out here was his way of showing his winged friend he was willing to receive a message.

He spotted her gliding, the glowing clouds as a backdrop. She wasn't flapping her wings but was saving her strength. Suddenly she accelerated, swooping toward him at over twice her gliding speed. As she descended, she gracefully slowed down and Wolfpaw stood frozen, to not disturb her approach. She effortlessly floated closer and Wolfpaw took in her entire wingspan, over four feet across he figured, then she was on his shoulder and both of them remained still. He had been opening himself while walking out here and felt ready for whatever she wanted to tell him.

It wasn't a long exchange, nor did it have to be. The choices for her and her kind were to leave the valley, long before the time to head to the warm, or to join in the fight, not accept this death that was now being thrust upon everyone.

There was fear in the message, but also anger. Wolfpaw felt a vague relief and even pride that the fury was not directed at him.

Wolfpaw did all he could to center his mind so that his thoughts were not cloudlike but more like a rock or mineral that he could hold out to be taken.

This is not right, he told her. *Humans have been killed who have nothing to do with the poison. I know you need to strike back but you also need to be sure. Killing for the sake of killing will not be good for anyone.*

Then come up to the mountains, she told him. *Talk to the one who is preparing us for battle.*

The hawk pushed off from his shoulder, making a hissing sound that reminded Wolfpaw of a louder version of his old kettle on the stove at home.

And now Wolfpaw was scared all over again. He didn't

want to go up to the mountains. He wanted to leave the valley altogether.

CHAPTER 6

Angie Prez was sitting on Ginger Kincaid's back porch, sipping the lemonade that Ginger had prepared. There were crackers too, and some cheddar slices and pretzels, all of which were practically untouched. Ginger had gone through the motions of hosting, but this wasn't exactly a social occasion. In a pants suit, Angie was dressed more casually than at Frank Kincaid's funeral. Ginger was wearing a cut-off sweatshirt, faded jeans and scuffed up running shoes.

Angie was a lawyer, specializing in labor law. Many, perhaps too many, of her cases were pro bono. She also headed the Colorado Earth Angels, a watchdog group that largely consisted of Angie blogging about environmental issues on the Internet. When she was a young activist, one of the first times Angie had her name in the paper, the writer had dropped the first 'e' and Angie found she preferred it to 'Perez' her legal name. In the early days of her practice, she'd been known as 'Key-ring Angie', the go-to counsel to spring local activists out of jail.

Angie looked at the tire-swing hanging from a towering cottonwood and pictured Frank on an afternoon like this, securing the rope to the tree. Ginger seemed nervous and not all that friendly, yet Angie knew it was time to get on with what she'd come here to discuss.

"Did you read those attachments I sent?"

"I looked at them."

"Frank worked an all-night shift, the night before he died. Wasn't that unusual?"

"He told me they were behind on production, and had to step it up in order to meet the demands of the schedule."

Angie took a moment. She picked up a pretzel, then simply held it without putting it in her mouth. "Did you have a sense that they may have been producing something out of the ordinary?"

"What do you mean?"

"The emissions from the plant appear to have intensified for more than two months now, ever since the middle of March. Did Frank ever mention there was a change in what they were producing?"

"No, he never said anything like that."

This exchange was proving more difficult than Angie had anticipated. She set the pretzel she'd been holding onto the small plate in front of her. "A number of people heard an explosion at the plant in the middle of the night during that shift Frank was working. Powerful enough to wake them up."

"Well, he died here at home."

"Okay, but maybe something extreme took place. Maybe he was exposed to something at Mentex that induced his heart failure."

"Frank always had a cough," Ginger replied. "Terrible allergies. I'm sure the firefighting didn't help."

"Let's assume nothing extreme happened at the plant that night – that it was business as usual. The symptoms you're describing have been identified in twenty-nine other cases in Boulder County. Sixteen of those people either worked at, or are still working at, Mentex. The rest lived in close proximity. Did Frank ever receive treatment for respiratory problems?"

Ginger shook her head. "You want some more lemonade, Angie?"

"No thank you. I suspect that, like those I just mentioned, Frank had an abnormal build-up of fluid in his lungs from exposure to elevated levels of nitrogen oxide, the kind of emissions that have been pouring out of Mentex." Angie looked at Ginger who was looking away. "We need to prove that your husband's death was due to conditions at the plant. To do that you'll need to file a wrongful death, civil suit against the company. That could light the spark for a class action suit involving every Mentex facility in the country, and maybe even around the globe."

"Will I have to testify?"

Angie looked back at her. "Of course. The whole case will unfold from the strength of your sworn deposition. If we go forward, and I hope you'll decide to do so, you'll need to be willing to go all the way. And I won't kid you, Mentex won't just roll over. They've got all the money in the world and there's a lot at stake for them."

There was a moment and Angie became aware of sounds she'd not been picking up on. Wind through the trees, birds trilling; the low hum of some machine in the distance.

"I think Frank just pushed himself too hard," said Ginger, her voice sounding flat and faraway.

"I know this is difficult."

"It is," uttered Ginger. "*Very* difficult."

Angie looked into Ginger's eyes, which, behind her glasses, were glistening with tears.

"You owe this to your daughters and yourself, and to Frank's memory, to determine once and for all whether what's being produced at Mentex is what killed him."

"What good is it going to do?" Ginger's voice sounded hollow, distant.

"At the very least, it might make them change their practices. Give you and hundreds, maybe thousands of others adversely affected some reasonable compensation. Make Mentex and everyone else in this region see that nobody, not even a powerful multi-national, can get away with murder. Don't you want justice for Frank?"

Ginger seemed to draw even further in. "This is too much. I can't deal with this right now."

She stood and gathered up the uneaten snacks before heading into the house.

CHAPTER 7

Todd always waited until the last minute to pack. He had acquired the tendency during the years he worked in Hollywood, promoting regional openings for the studio. He'd work an itinerary that resembled a rock tour, deifying the latest would-be blockbuster to the local scribes. They called it promotion but Todd had, in those days, come to think of himself as more of a political advance man, paving the way for the candidate (the film itself) to come to town. He got used to hotel rooms, albeit five star ones; living out of a suitcase, traveling light. He'd married into the industry, his wife Rene was a line producer with an eye toward becoming a director. Her father had been a celebrated director himself, Marvin Gower, credits stretching back to the sixties. Todd had always felt that Marvin vaguely disapproved of him, dismissing him as merely a guy who promoted any kind of chattel the studio was looking to sell, which Todd grudgingly acknowledged to be close to the truth.

Rummaging his bedroom closet for the shoes he'd bought while he and Rene were in Rome, he came across a picture in an empty shoebox. Todd remembered vividly the day it was taken. Like now, he'd been packing, preparing to get to LAX when Rene had rushed into their Santa Monica bungalow looking for her .35 millimeter Canon. "Come out front, come outside," she insisted as she darted from one room to another. She grabbed the camera from atop the bedroom chest and Todd followed her out into the morning, where there was a rainbow gleaming above, like a celestial horseshoe. "Stand there in the middle of the street, and I'll take your picture."

"Why don't you stand there," Todd had resisted, "you're the one who spotted it."

"Just stand in the middle and smile."

Todd did, and that was the picture, not of his gorgeous wife

27

whose smile was more dazzling than any rainbow, but he by himself, looking vaguely put upon, unshaven, wearing a t-shirt and sweats.

The following day, with Todd in Atlanta singing the dubious praises of *Cool Dudes III,* Rene was suddenly, incomprehensibly, run over by a sixteen-year-old who, while texting, veered off Pico Boulevard and onto the sidewalk.

Todd took a leave from the studio, which cross-faded to permanence. Sam Tolliver, his producer friend, had invested in a cigar company in the Dominican Republic and Todd's job for the next five years was promoting the joys of puffing on impeccably cured leaves and seeds. Todd was not a smoker himself, except for twice a year, Rene's April birthday and their November wedding anniversary. Wherever he was, meeting retail shop owners or wholesale dealers or editors and writers of men's publications, he would steal an hour on those two annual occasions to sit alone in a comfortable chair or on a scenic hillside and light up a *Presidente,* their top-of-the-line offering. It would soothe and somehow empower him, although, when the gray-white ash had burned to just above the ring, Todd would invariably shed the tears he'd been holding back for half-year intervals.

In Monterrey, speaking to a gathering of Mexico's *cap-i-tans de industry,* Todd impressed audience member and Mentex V.P. Jaime Ortega enough to be hired without an interview, at nearly twice what he was making. He'd fronted celluloid dreams and finely cured smoke, why not something tangible and necessary, like cement? Todd knew little about how it was made, nor did he care. What Todd knew was what he'd always had a flare for: convincing others that he represented something that would somehow enhance their lives.

For Mentex, his work had been exclusively at corporate headquarters, generating and revising copy on web pages and managing electronic correspondence. He hadn't engaged much with the company or with Mexico City. He had felt, for the past year-and-a-half, he was actively awaiting the next chapter of his life. He'd become restless, and that was what the transfer request was about.

Todd had grown accustomed to the fact that people needed cement and the by-products that Mentex provided, but didn't always want the messiness inherent in the process. You couldn't melt down elements without some of the effects billowing into the air. That's what it took to pave roads and driveways and sidewalks. Todd sometimes wondered if that sidewalk on Pico where Rene breathed her last had been paved with Mentex cement.

For this Colorado assignment he would need to assess the situation, then possibly implement damage control. Todd would get the job done for Sandoval and get himself assigned someplace he could use as a crow's nest to spot a sail on the horizon. That's how he saw himself since Rene's death: drifting, rudderless, in motion but going nowhere.

Todd glanced down and spotted his shoes, the ones he'd been looking for, on the floor in the corner. For an instant, he thought about tearing up the rainbow photo, but placed it back in the shoebox.

* * *

During the flight, Todd had his laptop open, reviewing the Mentex website. Under a heading titled: *Standards and Practices* it said: "*Mentex has a commitment, wherever it operates, to comply with the letter of the law. Any company who fails to do so undermines its mission, which should be to make an enduring contribution to the community it directly serves, as well as to the world at large.*" That second sentence, Todd recalled, was all his. Better to go general and express a platitude when referencing areas potentially troublesome to the company. As he scanned the content, the words *sustainable* and *sustainability*, as well as *responsible* and *responsibility*, and *transparent* and *transparency*, were salt-and-peppered throughout. Under *Health and Safety*, there was assurance that Mentex's operations were constantly being internally monitored, evaluated and improved. Todd sighed, knowing that eight years before, the company had to pay the state of Colorado one-point-six million for an array of clean-air violations at their Lynton plant.

At the Mentex–Lynton home page, as his eyes scanned the content, he was freshly reminded of an impression he'd filed away the first time he'd seen it. There were more images of, and references to, Lowell Felker than to any other Mentex plant manager in their entire operation. Perhaps it was just that Lynton was such a small community, but there were pictures of Lowell, not only in reference to the workings of the plant, but him hosting a pumpkin pie festival, him onstage, emceeing the Mentex Music Fest, even him judging a duck race at the Lynton Community Fair.

Todd exited that page and typed in a search: *Mentex, Lynton, community*. A site attributed to the Colorado Earth Angels, reported that Mentex's one-hundred-fifty employees were producing nearly a million tons of cement per year. It also reported (accurately) that the Lynton plant generated 5.4 million pounds of nitrogen oxide annually, as opposed to a single car's emission of 38.2 pounds. A lawyer/activist named Angie Prez, identified as the founder and chairperson of the organization stated: *"That's like an extra one-hundred-thirty-thousand cars per year rolling along Highway 64. It's outrageous."* It went on to report that the plant's kiln system boiled fresh limestone and other substances at 3,300 degrees emitting a plume of coal exhaust visible for miles. Ms. Prez was quoted throughout. *"You know when you're getting closer to Lynton; you can see it and you can smell it. And for the most part, the people in that area have no idea what exactly is in the air, or what effect it's having."*

Todd sighed again. He had his work cut out for him.

He was about to shut down his laptop when he saw *Three Killed in Bear Attack at Home.*

Todd read through the bizarre and alarming account. The mayor of the town he was going to, along with his college-age son and the son's fiancé were ravaged in the middle of the night when a bear wandered into the mayor's mountain home. The disturbing piece ended with a quote from Cinda Rigg, an Animal Control officer from the township: *"People are under the impression that Colorado is a safe and civilized environment. Tragically, that's not always the case."*

* * *

At baggage claim, Todd eyed the revolving belt for the two large bags he'd brought with him. One was kelly-green; the other, royal blue. Ugly yes, but easy to spot. There was the blue one now, tumbling down the chute. As he was stepping forward to grab it, a voice said, "Let me get that for you, Mr. Wendt." Todd looked over to see a tall guy with slicked-back black hair, around twenty, hoisting the bag from the belt. "Is this all?" the kid asked.

"No, there's that green one that just came down."

"On it," said the kid, and he hustled over as it swung around the bend. He was back in a breeze. "I'm Vance Dickason. How was the flight?"

"Flights," Todd said. "We had to change planes in Houston."

"Well, you're here now, although we've got a little ride ahead of us. But it's an Escalade, so you'll be comfortable."

They were walking, Vance carrying a bag on either side.

Todd glanced over. "I can take one of those."

"Wouldn't hear of it, Mr. Wendt."

"You work with Mentex, I take it."

"I work *with* Mentex, but I work *for* Lowell Felker. The boss is really looking forward to meeting you. Cleared a whole hour, first thing tomorrow morning. Boss doesn't do that for just anybody."

It was after nine, fully dark outside, the June air close and warm. The SUV, black and gleaming, was waiting for them in a premier spot in short-term parking. Vance opened the nearest back door for Todd, then set both bags in the rear.

As Todd settled in, Vance said, "That little fridge is fully stocked. You might want some water on account of the altitude here. If you're hungry, the sandwiches are awesome. Meat and vegetarian, both."

"I'm fine," said Todd.

Vance eased out of the parking lot, then passed an arrow indicating the airport exit up ahead. In the distance, Denver was glowing. But they were soon headed in the opposite direction, toward the looming mountains and further into the darkness. There were several miles of toll-way, followed by as many miles of interstate, then dark, two-lane Highway 64, interrupted only by the northernmost edge of Valmont.

"Not much out here," said Todd, breaking the silence.

"Lynton's a little further west. We'll pass the plant on the way into town."

And so they did, although all Todd could see as they drove beneath an arching bridge over the highway was the Mentex sign and a security wall protecting a dense tree line; a cluster of remote, towering spheres pushing up behind everything.

"We have the same security grid they used to have at Rocky Flats."

"What's Rocky Flats?" asked Todd.

"A nuclear power plant. Used to be, until the tree-huggers caused it to close. How long have you been with Mentex?"

"A year and a half," said Todd. "Why d'you ask?"

"Most of the execs I pick up are Mexican, or else they're old pals of Mr. Felker's from Texas. Are you from out east or something?"

"Chicago. Oak Park, actually. Like Hemingway."

"Who?" Vance asked.

They were at a stoplight that effectively marked the beginning of Lynton. As they pushed into town, Vance offered a few comments on the real estate. They passed the Pump It Up filling station and Quik Mart, the only establishment in town that stayed open all night. They passed one of the town's three liquor stores as well as one of its four marijuana facilities, then a dismal laundromat and a gaudy nail salon. As 64 split and transformed to the commercial strip known as North Center Street, they passed the China Palace, as well as Spokes Bicycle Shop and a few galleries and antique stores.

"Kind of looks like a movie set, doesn't it, Mr. Wendt? This is a big stopping place for families headed up to Rocky Mountain National Park. Quaint, is how a lot of people refer to it."

They turned left at the end of North Center Street and went only a block or so until Vance steered the Escalade right, onto a dirt road that led to a series of similar looking wooden structures.

"You'll be staying in a development we have along the river. It was a company investment, meant to be affordable housing, especially for our own employees, but most of them have opted to remain where they are, either in town or in Valmont. So they're available for execs like you while you're working here. Right on the river, and adjacent to the park. You're gonna love it, Mr. Wendt."

They pulled up and Todd got out and once again offered to help Vance with the bags but the kid insisted on hauling them into the cottage-like residence himself.

Wood everywhere, spacious and open, with high-beamed ceilings. The kitchen was on the left, a full entertainment area in the spacious living room and a small downstairs bathroom. Upstairs was a loft with a master bedroom and bath, the bedroom overlooking the river, with the open expanse of the public park and campgrounds beyond.

Vance left and Todd climbed the railed wooden stairs that led to the bedroom loft. He stood near the expansive glass window and looked out at the darkness, listening to the rush of the river below. It would be, he knew, beautiful out there in the morning.

He sat on the edge of the bed and was thinking of heading back down to retrieve one of the suitcases and start to unpack, but he leaned back and closed his eyes and the murmur of the river sang him to sleep.

CHAPTER 8

Cinda was clutching a note that had been left for her at the station. She looked down and freshly read the child like scrawl.

To the Lady Officer
I wanted to tell you this all ready – warn you – but didnt have at that time information that I have. Because of what is hapenning – the air and trees and water being poisoned like they are – things are going to get worst. You know Mentex is what I speak of. My creature friends are being forced to strike back and strike back harsh. I am telling you this because you are a good person whose treated me good. I do not want to be a round when all of what will happen will be hapenning. I hope only the ones guilty are hurt – that they are going to start with them.
Fair well, Wolfpaw

Cinda stared at the letter. She wondered if maybe she'd given Wolfpaw too much credit; maybe he was crazy after all. But Wolfpaw knew more about what was going on under the surface of Lynton with both its humans and non-humans than anybody. Slightly unsettled, she slipped the letter back into its envelope, opened her drawer and placed it inside.

* * *

Wolfpaw awoke as dawn was spreading over the mountains. His time up here had reinforced the feeling that his senses, keen though they were, were in need of sharpening. Years of floating among the same surroundings in Lynton had allowed a kind of softness to settle into his spirit. What most in civilization would regard as primitive instincts, were the ones he needed to renew.

There were silver-blue clouds and it looked like it might

finally rain today. Rain was needed, in the mountains and in the valley. Wolfpaw had been extra vigilant, especially during his daytime excursions, for any sign of fire. Given the parched condition of the earth, a fire could be devastating.

Standing there, sipping the cinnamon water he'd heated by the fire, his scratched and dented metal cup still warm in his hand, Wolfpaw's eyes caught the sweep of the red-tailed hawk, dipping from above, the one he'd communicated with that night among the open fields. He'd not seen her until now, but felt at times she was in proximity, concealing herself, yet watching him with a kind of detached vigilance.

Then, from the distant ground, a glint of something else in the rising dawn. He lowered his eyes and probed the bowl of the sagging valley. He couldn't detect anything and was about to release his gaze when he caught a beige form gliding through the high weeds.

It was a lion, a large one, a hundred fifty pounds or more. Wolfpaw wondered if it was the same one he'd seen twice in town; once striding across the road that ran along the river, once crossing the field that lay between Burnham Park and the high school. From front paws to the end of its tail, it had spanned every inch of the road. The tail had been thick as the thickest tent rope. Its spirit suggested a kind of brutal intelligence and seemed to project not only that sixth sense that so many creatures had, but a seventh sense as well, one that even a human as attuned as Wolfpaw was not able to fathom. If the lion was aware of Wolfpaw's presence, it was not in any way concerned as it slipped through a clearing, appearing to be headed toward some point on the face of the mountain.

Wolfpaw's eyes traced a trajectory from the lion to the orange-red rocks. Then he saw something else: an elk, a huge bull, easily eight hundred pounds, with an enormous rack, approaching from the foot of the mountain straight toward the lion. It was proceeding slowly, evenly measured steps, but no fear or timidity in its motion. Wolfpaw drew a breath as, from the top of his sight, he now took in the gleaming black coat of a massive bear, winding swiftly toward the lion. Then finally something else: a silver-coated coyote loping up from the foreground.

The lion had halted in a dry creek basin at the mountain's base. The four creatures were converged there, having arrived from all directions. Whatever communication was taking place was being conducted by the lion, for the others were acceding to him, their eyes keen upon their leader. Then their attention shifted, and not just the lion, but each of the creatures was unmistakably looking in his direction.

No, not in his direction, looking at *him*.

He fought the urge to turn his back, leave his rations and resources, and put as much distance between himself and the situation as possible. His other sense, the Over-sense that hovered around all of his perceptions, told him he was not only being looked at, but called to. The lion, at least, had known where Wolfpaw was all along.

Four pairs of eyes were staring, waiting; not only beckoning, but pulling him. It was not friendly, nor was it hostile. What it possessed was an unmistakable power and purpose. They didn't need Wolfpaw, but they wanted him. They were offering that he could be, if not of them, then somehow with them, a fellow spirit who could play a role in the war they had been forced to wage.

Wolfpaw stopped his mind. Now was not the time to think. He drew a breath, then took his first step down the slope to join them.

* * *

As Wolfpaw was admitted to the tight circle at the foot of the mountain, the hawk floated down to rest on his shoulder and convey the messages between the creatures and Wolfpaw. What they wanted to know for certain was which humans made the poison clouds that would billow out of the smokestacks, and who was bringing the new death-fire up from the ground, poisoning the air and soil and water. The creatures could not drink the water in the valley, and the air singed their eyes and noses and throats. The humans didn't seem to feel it as strongly as they did, but it was getting worse with each sunset.

Wolfpaw said he would point the way for them, identify the humans who were most responsible. The message to stop needed to be sent, but in ways that did not result in human death, Wolfpaw not wanting that blood to stain his soul.

When it became clear what he was telling them, the other creatures – the elk, the bear, the coyote – looked to the lion, and the lion, for what felt like years to Wolfpaw, did not respond. There was finally a change in his eyes, like the moment when night passes to dawn, and Wolfpaw knew, and the other creatures knew, that the lion had reluctantly agreed.

But Wolfpaw also knew it wasn't settled. He felt he already knew who had to be tagged but needed to be certain. Things could go wrong and he could not shake the look he'd seen in the eyes of the lion. The creature was only going along because he needed Wolfpaw. It would be better for the creatures to target a few humans rather than strike out against a whole town. But this plan wouldn't last forever. If anything shifted, if the humans in question did anything other than heed these final warnings, flesh would be torn and blood would flow and lives would be lost as swiftly and strongly as the river that ran through the heart of Lynton.

CHAPTER 9

Beyond the expansive bedroom window, Juniper Park sprawled out green and lush. The royal-blue sky was brushed with blotches of vivid, white clouds, but it was the mountains that took Todd's breath away, imposing and towering, their red clay faces beaming down on the town of Lynton.

Todd partially unpacked, taking out only what he needed to shower and shave and prepare for what he knew would be an important day. The water took a while to get hot but then it was steaming and proved to be a challenge to cool down.

He chose a casual look, a short-sleeved, pale-blue shirt and khaki slacks and argyles, over which he slipped a pair of cordovan loafers, then changed his mind and put on his dark-blue Reeboks. He was going to walk to the plant and wanted to be comfortable. Every promotional picture he'd ever seen of Lowell Felker never included a suit and tie.

There was a pristine coffee-maker and an unopened bag of Starbuck's French Roast but although Todd never started the morning without caffeine, he grabbed his laptop and ventured out.

The sun was already intense, even for eight-fifteen in the morning. He slipped on his black-rimmed shades and started walking in the opposite direction he and Vance had taken into town. He passed the town hall with the sheriff's office adjacent to it. Across the street was an ancient, converted train depot which served as the town library, and further down the block was a recycling station with three massive bins. A couple who looked to be in their seventies were dutifully depositing their items: he, the glass and plastic: she, the cardboard and paper. Todd was increasingly awake as he passed through a small, tidy park with a band shell and a visitor's center.

He waited at a corner on South Center Street, whose traffic

went one way, east, away from the mountains. A few cars passed, then he crossed into a parking lot in front of the Citizens' Bank and a small complex of doctor's offices. Beyond and to the right was North Center Street. There he saw the details of what had been merely shadows the night before – galleries, antiques, the bike shop, the flower shop, the ice-cream parlor, the wine and liquor store, the pizza joint, the drugstore, the grocery – a curious blend of local tradition and gentrification. The street beyond, to the left, looked like it also might have some activity but that was pretty much the town. Besides, Todd spotted exactly what he was looking for, *The Wagging Tail: coffee and baked goods*.

A group of men, whom Todd assumed to be retirees, were taking up the only large table. Scattered about the coffee shop were other patrons, a few with laptops, a few reading newspapers, some talking. Todd ordered a shot-in-the-dark from the pink-haired and liberally pierced young woman behind the counter. "Want anything to go along with that? We just took a bunch of scones out of the oven."

"Just the coffee, thanks."

Todd seated himself near the back, having taken with him a *Lynton Weekly Record* someone had left on the counter.

The featured article was under the headline *Lynton to Select Interim Mayor*. Todd scanned the piece. There was a reference to *"the tragic and untimely death of former Mayor Ned Haddock,"* but no further details regarding the attack. The assumption seemed to be that anyone reading it was familiar with the story and didn't need to be reminded of its brutality. Other articles were about end-of-the-year activities at a few of the area schools, as well as a review of a recent anthology of cowboy poetry.

On page three Todd saw the headline: *Mentex Sponsors Annual Acoustic Music Fest*. Accompanying, was a picture of Lowell Felker flanked by a pair of local musicians; one male who looked like a teenager, identified as Barry Quinn, and one female who looked every bit a star, named Iris Avery. The festival, it said, would be held over the July fourth weekend and would feature *"the finest of the many fine musicians we are fortunate to have among us, as well as some amazing national attractions."* Felker went on to say: *"It's just another way that Mentex keeps giving back to the community."*

Todd leafed through the rest of the paper, mostly ads and calendar notices spread among special interest features: one about quilting, and one with tips about cooking buffalo chili. Todd finished the paper, then his coffee. Noting it was after nine o'clock, he stepped back out and headed toward the Mentex plant at the edge of town.

He passed the Pump It Up gas station, the last vestige of commercial real estate. At the point where Highway 38 and 64 intersected, the first leading to Boulder, the second to Valmont, he continued east.

Traffic was sparse as he trudged along the road, open fields on either side. On his right was a ditch, beyond which was a barbed-wire fence and a field populated with a herd of maybe twenty horses. Todd enjoyed being in a rural area with such ready evidence of domestic animals, figuring the fields that did not contain horses likely housed cattle, or even goats or sheep.

The blue sky was now practically cloudless. The sun was white gold: the forecast, for the mid-eighties. A flock of ten or twelve very large black birds appeared from his left, not that far above him. They passed overhead, then swung in a ninety degree loop, flapping and cawing in the opposite direction. *Crows, ravens?* Todd made a mental note to look them up on the web if he found some down time during the day.

As he continued walking, he sensed some movement in the brush, off to his right. He turned his head but there was merely the ditch, running parallel to his own steady progress, then some high weeds that gave way to a dense thicket. Still, he'd sensed something... Probably, he told himself, just some random shaft of light.

41

Getting closer to Mentex, Todd ran through his mind what he'd studied in preparation for coming to the plant. Shortly after the mid-nineteenth century, Elias Howard Lynton owned two hundred acres of what became the main section of the town that would bear his name. This included a limestone quarry as well as sandstone outcroppings. He was responsible for the first kiln, comprised of local sandstone and lined with firebrick. Limestone was quarried and burned in the kilns, generating a pink powder which, when blended with the local sand, approximated the singular hue that became known as Lynton Red Sandstone. This was the beginning of what ultimately defined Lynton as a quarry town, known for producing nearly two hundred bushels of lime each day. Elias died in 1881, an event that led to the establishment of a formal cemetery in Lynton, in which he was the first to be interred. Yet his industry continued and, as early as 1900, Lynton citizens vigorously objected to the pollution that spewed from the kilns. By the mid-twentieth century, the plant had exclusively become a cement-producing site.

Mentex was originally called Texament, based in Houston, which relocated to Mexico after the NAFTA agreement to escape the unions and take advantage of cheap labor. The company was sold to a Mexican conglomerate headed by the family of CEO Herman Sandoval. After Mentex acquired the plant in Lynton in the mid-1990s, much was made of Mentex's local legacy, while the international connection was downplayed.

There was substantial security at all Mentex facilities. Todd showed his employee ID and, as soon as he was admitted through the main gate, came upon a twelve-foot sandstone statue of Elias Howard Lynton that seemed to be overseeing the workings of the plant. Then he spotted Vance Dickason, clad in black shirt and slacks, on a cast-iron bench, fingers fluttering on his iPhone. "Hello there, Vance," Todd called over.

Vance stood up awkwardly. "Mr. Felker told me to text him as soon as you got here. He wants to come down and give you a personal tour."

"Just take me to his office, please."

Vance smiled, even more awkwardly. "The boss was really looking forward to showing you around himself, Mr. Wendt."

"Take me to his office, okay?"

Then the young man swung his right arm in an arc that almost slammed against Todd. Vance flailed his arm a few more times, then contorted to his right.

Taken aback, Todd saw what the young man was so frantically responding to: a wasp or a bee, some kind of yellow-black stinging insect, now fluttering away.

Vance's expression relaxed a bit. "Sorry about that, Mr. Wendt. If I get stung by one of those things, I'll go into serious shock." He smiled again, more naturally this time. "All right, then. If you insist, let's head up to Mr. Felker's office."

* * *

Lowell Felker was on the fourth floor of the red-stone and glass structure that housed Mentex's regional administrative offices. As Todd entered, he glimpsed a breathtaking view of the mountains to the west. He didn't savor it long, however, as Lowell rose, all six-three of him, behind his expansive, uncluttered, glass-topped desk. He beamed and in a booming voice, said, "You didn't need to come up, man, I was all set to come down. Great to meet you, heard so much about you. Your accommodations suit you? We've got you a car all lined up for you to use while you're here. Being detailed as we speak." All of this while vigorously pumping Todd's hand like Lowell was parched and expected to draw water from it.

Todd managed something that approached a smile but inwardly was cringing. He didn't enjoy shaking hands, felt it was a ridiculous custom. Plus, how many times had he shaken someone's hand only to be informed that they were feeling under the weather or were just getting over a cold or the flu? Moments like this, with individuals such as Lowell Felker, there was nothing to do but endure it.

Lowell released Todd's hand and indicated a leather couch. "Why don't you sit before we take our tour? You want you a bottled water or a soda or something? It's a little early for a cocktail." Lowell looked at Vance who was standing nearby. "Son, go get Mr. Wendt a ginger ale. We still got some Vernor's left, don't we?"

"If it's all the same, just show me where I'll be working."

Lowell's smile faded, then reconfigured itself into an expression meant to appear loose and breezy but which held some strain around the edges. "We figured you'd be spending most of your time out in the field. Didn't Sandoval send you down to smooth out the neighborhood tree-huggers?"

"Lowell, I'm sure you've got everything under control here. But when I assess a situation, I need to arrive at an overall perspective."

Lowell drifted back over to his desk as he gestured toward his assistant. "Well, all right, then. Vance, see that Mr. Wendt is set up in that corner office, on the ground floor. Get him whatever it is he thinks he needs." He beamed at Todd, his tiny eyes gleaming: "Now how's that grab you, partner?"

CHAPTER 10

At his request for an assistant, Todd was assigned Edna Murdoch, a pleasant woman in her late-sixties who'd been doing temporary office work at Mentex. She was scheduled to conclude her temp job that week, and seemed grateful to be held over. After Edna left, Todd worked into the night, growing accustomed to his sterile and very modest office.

He shut down just before midnight and headed home via North Center Street. Lynton did look like a movie set, especially at night. There was a dim glow from the next street over and Todd drifted toward it. Passing through a space between the drugstore and a generic, two-story office complex, he saw that the glow was from a place called *Ossie's Blues n' Brew*.

Todd couldn't determine if it was open. There was a single car in the parking lot, a Buick, well preserved but with a couple of decades on it. To reach the entrance, a set of wooden steps needed to be climbed as the establishment was set on top of a hill. Todd was at the front door now, a massive oak one that eased open as he pushed it with the heel of his hand. The place was dim, the most prominent color being the same blue glow emanating from outside.

A lone figure was standing behind the bar. Slight, and of medium height, he was dressed casually and wore a pair of glasses whose frames seemed over-sized. He had dark hair and skin and an expression that appeared to be amused by something. "You a beer drinker?" he asked, by way of a greeting.

"Sure," said Todd.

"I need you to taste something for me."

A pair of tall cans stood on the bar and the man filled two short, thick glasses with contents from each. "This first one," said the barman, "I call Bitches Brew, although I'll probably change the name if I go public with it. Take a taste and hold your thoughts about it."

Todd held it up and looked closely at it, squinting due to the lack of light. The head was still settling. He swirled the liquid in the glass, pulled the glass close to his face and smelled it, a caramel-like aroma filling his nostrils. Todd took a sip, savoring the liquid on his tongue, breathing through it. He was no expert but he'd been to a couple of beer tastings and had consumed plenty in his day, from all over the world. This was stout, thick and complicated. He could imagine drinking one glass of it but probably not a second.

"Here," the barman said, "take a sip of water and clear your pipes."

Todd did so. The barman was taking this all quite seriously and Todd was responding in kind. "Now this other one," the guy said, "is my latest concoction. See if it grabs you."

Todd held the small glass up to make the most of what light was available. The shade was black as ink but somehow didn't look as thick as the first one. When he swirled it, the liquid appeared silky, circling the glass. It smelled like fine perfume. Todd took a taste. Lighter, smoother, less complex, much easier on the tongue, and it literally caressed the inside of the mouth. He took another sip and breathed through it before letting it slide back in his throat. Not silk, but velvet, definitely velvet. "Wow, what do you call this one?"

The barman beamed a mixture of pride and relief. "Ossie's Ebony Ale. That's the one, isn't it?"

"I'd say so. What are you going to do, serve it here, on draft?"

"That, and send it off in the morning to the New York Times Sunday Magazine. They're holding a competition for the best micro in America and I figured I'd take a shot."

"How do you submit it?"

"Exactly the way I'll sell it – in a tall aluminum can. I've had the can designed for weeks but this is the first time I've gotten the taste just right. I've been stockpiling water from Eldorado

Springs, just south of Boulder. You really did like it, correct, you're not blowing smoke?"

"Why would I? It's terrific."

The barman laughed. "If I lose I'm holding you responsible. I'm Ossie, by the way, welcome to my place. Now, let's sit here and have a drink, you and me. I didn't hear you pull up, so I'm assuming you're not driving, right?"

* * *

Ossie Anderson had been in Lynton twenty years. He'd moved to Denver from Newark with his wife, Lil, and their four kids, and initially opened a furniture restoration business. "You know why so many black people ended up in Newark?" Ossie asked Todd that first night. "They were coming up from the South on those trains headed for New York, and when the conductor called out 'Newark' a lot of them misheard and thought he was saying 'New York' and that's where they got off."

Upon moving to Lynton, work proved to be steady but slow. So he got into another line, opening Ossie's Roadhouse across from the stone quarry at the entrance to town. Five years after that he established Ossie's Blues n' Brew in a deserted warehouse on Summit Street, the only other significant vessel through Lynton. He started brewing his own beer after the Coors and Budweiser distributors kept gouging him. The place was big enough that he also ran music upstairs. Ossie was a jazz aficionado, especially the be-bop era of Miles and Trane and Monk. With not enough local jazz to support a nightly music card, he turned to blues. Besides, his clientele was almost exclusively white and Ossie felt that white folks loved the blues, especially when they were playing it. They also loved bluegrass, a form that Ossie had no regard for whatsoever, but the town was lousy with that type of music, had indeed become some kind of a haven for it, so Sunday afternoon through Wednesday night the blues faded to bluegrass, hosted by Iris Avery who'd grown up in Valmont and had lived in Nashville for a few years, co-writing one hit for Faith Hill and singing back-up on a couple of others. Several years back she'd won first prize in the women's division of Marty Stewart's National Mandolin Contest held in Bean Blossom, Indiana.

Ossie loved baseball, was a Yankee fan, "You might as well go with what's classic," and listened to every game of theirs he could on satellite radio. He also sponsored a local team, Ossie's Brewers, who played a couple of times a week over at Burnham Park on the south side of town.

Todd found out all of this and more in the hours he and Ossie sat in the neon shadows of *Ossie's Blues n' Brew*. Ossie had a quarter century on Todd but also a youthful exuberance, an engaging mixture of enthusiasm with a hint of cynicism. They drank steadily but slowly and neither man seemed visibly intoxicated. While Todd hadn't anticipated any all-night conversations in Lynton, what the hell, Lowell Felker had made it clear that Todd was pretty much on his own at Mentex.

* * *

When Todd left Ossie's, it wasn't yet dawn but the sky had that deep gray luminance of morning peeking from under the covers. He felt buzzed from the beer and warmed by the feeling that he'd found a new place and made a new friend.

He crossed the empty parking lot and came to Highway 38, which resumed once it was no longer interrupted by North Center Street. The highway commenced with a slight rise, as though confirming that it led further into the mountains. A green reflecting sign with silver letters signaled the way to Rocky Mountain National Park. Todd walked on the left side, against the traffic, although none was approaching.

When he reached the intersection where North Center Street

ended; the drugstore on one corner, the market across the way, a truck rolled up and Todd waited for it to pass. He crossed the street, then the parking lot behind the market and came to the other of Lynton's two Center Streets, this one also going one-way, but in the opposite direction.

There was an open area to Todd's left and he smelled the mix of fragrances from an array of trees and shrubbery. Todd's senses were slightly dulled from the beer but he was alert enough to notice some glint of movement.

He looked across the grass and, forty to fifty yards away, a dog was loping toward a row of bushes, its coat gray and sleek in the pressing light. But the motion was unusual and Todd instinctively knew this was a wild creature, a large fox or a coyote. It reached the bushes and didn't emerge from the other side and Todd, who had stopped, was consumed with the feeling that the animal, now hidden among the low branches, was gazing back at him.

Todd was surprised it had not continued in the direction it was heading, but had halted, training its eyes on him from across the park. Todd resumed walking, still attuned to the animal lurking behind him in the distance. Again, no traffic, and this time, when Todd reached the middle of Peach Orchard Road, which ran in front of where Todd was staying, he turned and saw it slink out of the bushes and cross the frontage road that ran by the library and the police station.

It was a coyote, no doubt about it, and again, rather than avoiding Todd's gaze, it appeared to be looking back at him, clearly aware it had been spotted but not overtly unsettled by it. Perhaps, Todd thought, the proximity to so much untamed terrain made the coyotes bolder in these parts, more accustomed to rubbing shoulders with the populace. Maybe it was rabid, although it appeared vital and healthy and totally at ease as it kept its eyes on Todd and loped across Peach Orchard Road.

It passed to the other side of the set of cottages, apparently on its way to the open space of Juniper Park, which led to the foot of the mountain. Clear of the road, Todd was now on the gravel drive leading up to his residence. The carport was on the left and he spotted the bronze Malibu the company had dropped off the day before. He'd yet to turn over the engine.

In the few minutes it had taken Todd to walk home, the sky had steadily been peeling open and now there was abundant silver adorning the dark blue. He reached into his jacket and pulled out his keys, grasping them in his palm, then he stopped.

The coyote was there on the gravel, staring, seemingly challenging him as it imposed itself between him and his front door.

The animal's coat was silver as the sky and its eyes were piercing blue. It appeared bigger than when he'd seen it from a distance and its coat had seemed deeper in shade. Todd was struggling to manage his growing confusion when he noted movement beyond the coyote that was staring him down.

Approaching was another coyote and Todd realized it was the one who'd been tracking him in the park. He backed up slowly, keeping his eyes on the closer one, but stopped again as he heard a low sound.

He glanced behind. Ten yards away was a third coyote, this one darker still; as large as the one in front of him. Todd froze. He couldn't go forward; couldn't go back. The original coyote, the smaller, gray one, was now flanking the big one in front, fanning out to Todd's left, placing a further barrier were Todd bold enough to attempt to dash to his front door. He suddenly wished he hadn't had anything to drink; he was going to need all the awareness he could summon.

On his front porch, another coyote appeared, bounding down the steps, blocking any move toward the entrance. This one was pale with a rust-colored shade to its coat.

Todd sensed another presence, heard another sound and couldn't help it, he wheeled around and there were two others.

That made six, completing a loose but effective circle, ten or twelve feet in diameter, with Todd at its center.

The growling was intermittent, erupting here and there as though a ball of hostility were being tossed among Todd's oppressors. He suppressed a sound rising from deep within, pushing it back from his throat to his gut. He couldn't determine whether it was a scream or a hysterical laugh.

Todd was suddenly back in high school, freshman year. He'd stayed late for band practice, rehearsing for an upcoming concert, stepping out of the rear entrance to the school, trumpet case in one hand, book bag in the other, only to come upon a group of older guys, the ones he'd seen smoking in the parking lot during lunch hour, who would routinely shake down fellow students for whatever they could get. They even made some kids fork over their car keys so they could cruise around town while the hapless owners were stuck in class. They must have had after-school detention together as it was just past dark. Why they were still hanging around Todd didn't know, but as he was confronted with several sets of unfriendly eyes, one of them said, "Well, well, what have we here?"

Todd had frozen then like he was frozen now, knowing that walking further into the group was risky and dangerous. Back then, he'd simply stopped, walked backward and opened the door, returning into the school to rush down the hallway and out the main entrance. He hadn't been pursued and that was the extent of the encounter. He'd berated himself long afterwards for running away, but was grateful he'd come up with a course of non-action that kept him from getting battered. But here there was no door to back into, no hallway to rush down; no front entrance that meant freedom; he was literally in the middle of something foreign and bizarre, from which there was no escape.

There was a blur on his right side and he spun toward it. A pair of jaws snapped an inch from his wrist. Then, a flash to his left as another lunged, snapping its jaws in the same way.

The one in front, the silver-coated alpha, leaped forward and nipped at Todd's kneecap, tearing his pants in one swift slash.

From behind, one tore at his elbow, viciously ripping the fabric of his shirt.

The one on the steps bounded toward him and, in mid-air, snapped it teeth. Todd felt its muzzle brush harshly across his nose and mouth.

While none of them followed through on these actions, Todd felt that each was just a prelude to his being dragged to the ground and torn to pieces.

His heart was throbbing, the veins in his neck coursing as though he were running at full speed. His arms felt weak and useless. He'd never been in quicksand but his legs felt like they were bound by some powerful force he could not identify... He'd have to fight back. If he could just scare off one of them, a kick to the ribs or a blow to the snout, the others might see that he was not going without a struggle, that perhaps he was more trouble than it was worth.

The silver alpha was easing forward, not cautiously, but boldly. Todd sensed the others closing in, the circle tightening. This was it. *Stop thinking, just react.* They were a few feet away, snarling and pressing in from every side. *This couldn't be happening.* And yet it was; he was about to be mauled and torn apart.

There was a loud crack and time froze. The silver alpha tilted his head back, appearing to sniff the air. Another crack, and this time the alpha spun away from Todd – bounding toward the open field, the mountains in front of him, the pack dashing behind.

Todd stood, his unbelieving eyes watching the coyotes as they retreated. Then he turned and saw a uniformed figure standing there, revolver in hand.

Officer Cinda Rigg, flushed and wide-eyed, looked only a little less relieved than Todd. In her Auckland accent she breathlessly declared, "I'd say that was a helluva spot."

Todd tried to speak but nothing came out.

Cinda put her gun back in its holster. "I was just driving by, about to end my shift."

Finding some breath, he said, "Have you ever come upon a whole pack like that?"

Cinda shook her head. "Heard them, never seen more than two at once," she told him.

They stood a moment, like they were both recovering from some kind of mad sprint. Then Todd said, "My name's Todd Wendt. I just got to town... I work at Mentex."

"Cinda Rigg, Animal Control." She gave a shaky laugh. "I guess I earned my pay tonight."

Todd laughed. "Thank God you did." Exhausted and shaken, Todd turned and walked

toward his place.

Cinda returned to her SUV. She'd never fired her gun before and was relieved she'd done so without any bloodshed. But as she climbed behind the wheel, a phrase from Wolfpaw's letter came back to her: *Mentex is what I am speaking of... My creature friends are being forced to strike back...*

CHAPTER 11

Lowell was in bed with Iris when his wife called. It wasn't unusual for him to be in bed with Iris, he arranged for that, every chance he could get. It was unusual that Myra would call twice in one week. She'd called on Monday and now it was only Thursday. He hoped something wasn't wrong with one of the kids. They were all out of school now, on their own; you'd think they could look after themselves.

"I need to take this," he told Iris. He usually turned off his cell but had been in too much of a hurry to get Iris undressed. She watched him languidly as he ducked into her bathroom. He closed the door and turned on both faucets in the sink in order to obscure his end of the conversation. "What's up?" Lowell said.

"You got a letter from the IRS," Myra told him.

A letter from Iris was how he heard it. "A letter from who?"

"IRS. The tax people. The government. Why didn't you tell me we owed back taxes?"

"I've got a lawyer working on it. A tax specialist... Everything all right on your end?"

"You should have told me."

"I was going to."

"When?"

"When I get back there."

"When is that going to be?"

"I'm trying to arrange it now. I've been all tied up."

A simmering pause. "Did you get the package?" asked Myra.

"What package?"

"One of those glass globes you've always liked. It's got real sand and cactus inside."

"I'll have Vance make sure it got delivered. The mail's been screwy."

"It might remind you that you still have a life back here. What are you going to do about this letter?"

"Just send it to me, and I'll— "

She hung up. Lowell turned off the running water.

He and Myra had married as UT undergraduates, their first child arriving five months later. Myra's father had made a fortune in aviation parts, and he'd never embraced Lowell. He and Myra would have divorced ten years ago but Myra had joined some Old Testament sect that believed divorces should only be granted if both partners stood before witnesses and testified as to what sins they had committed leading to the dissolution of the marriage. To his knowledge, Myra had never committed adultery, but Lowell had made a career of it. He wasn't about to stand up in front of anybody and admit, or for that matter deny, his infidelities. Confessing or lying after swearing on the Bible might mean that Myra would get the ranch, the stocks, everything. He wished he hadn't caved in to her father when he was twenty-one and signed that pre-nup. Lowell was too old to be eating cat food in a furnished room somewhere. The moves he was making would ensure that would never happen.

He took a leak, then stepped back into the bedroom. Iris had her hands laced behind her head, lustrous blonde hair spread out beneath her. "Who was that, lover?" She smiled after she said it.

Lowell lifted the top sheet and eased in next to her. "Just Vance, wanting to know about some transportation for tomorrow."

Iris chuckled. "The hell it was."

Lowell rose up beside her, trying to look at ease. "Darlin', you're not turning suspicious on me are you?"

She got out of bed, curves and swerves, gliding naked toward the bathroom. As she pulled the door open, she said. "I swear, Lowell, you're like a little boy who just put a rock through a picture window."

Lowell felt something turn in his stomach. Why the hell did he pick up that call? "It *was* Vance. You want me to call so you can talk to him yourself?"

"That boy would shit in his hat if you asked him to."

She stepped back into the bedroom, all five-foot-seven of her, with that body that kept him coming back. Flawless. She damn well knew it, too.

"You think I care, Lowell?"

"About what?"

She dove toward the bed and grabbed each of his wrists; she was strong as hell.

Iris bent forward, gazing into his eyes, smile still on her face. "You think I don't know you're married?"

"I didn't... we never talked about it."

"How dumb do you think I am? If I didn't know by you flying back to Texas every few weeks, it shows up in your Google search. Well, here's a news flash, lover: Iris doesn't give a rat."

Lowell felt a wave of confused relief rise up within him. Then he felt her lips and tongue and luscious mouth, moving down, down, down. "Lowell's got a wifey," she sang. "Lowell's got a wifey..."

"Stop it, Iris."

"Stop what – stop doing *this*?" Her hand took hold of his swelling cock. Iris laughed. "If you could get this anywhere else, Lowell, I'm pretty sure we wouldn't be here."

Lowell started to say something but as Iris kept going, he just emitted a low moan.

Iris pulled her head back and said, "And now that I've got your attention, Mr. Felker, there's something I need to ask you."

"What's that?" Lowell managed.

"You know what it is, 'cause I've asked you before."

"Oh no," Lowell uttered with a short laugh. "Not that again."

"Yes, that again." She gave a small laugh of her own and said, as she lowered herself once more, "You're gonna let me ride Comanche."

* * *

Four o'clock in the morning. Officer Cinda Rigg drove her white Ford Explorer along leafy, sleepy Third Street. She passed the Greening house. Jed Greening, a real estate developer and amateur archer, had been guzzling wine one evening and shot an arrow that stuck into the back of the Weymouth house across the way. It seemed amusing in retrospect but the fool could have killed somebody. Cinda vaguely realized she was easing toward the Lynton Cemetery. She usually checked it out at least once during her shift. There might be some kids up to mischief.

Her headlights probed the darkness, lighting up the gravestones. She recalled something her father said once, back in New Zealand, "The graveyards are filled with irreplaceable people."

Cinda hated to admit it, but graveyards freaked her out. That was all the more reason to make sure she didn't avoid this site during her nightly rounds. "Whatever you most fear should be confronted." Something else her father had said. He'd been an English instructor and Cinda was never sure which of his pronouncements were quotes and which he might have invented.

She was deeper into the cemetery now, the older part that ended with a hill pressing upwards. Against the hill, in the beams of her headlights, she sensed motion, strangeness, something out of the ordinary. She stopped the Explorer, then sat frozen in her seat when she realized what it was.

A mountain lion.

Long, sinewy, lying on the slope of the hill, gnawing at something. Probably a kill; a deer maybe, although Cinda didn't see anything in front of, or around it.

The lion rose with what struck her as impudent reluctance, glaring at her with gleaming yellow eyes, some indistinguishable mass clamped between its teeth. It swung around and then was up the hill in a single, powerful push.

Cinda exhaled, took a moment, then drove forward and got out of the car, pump action shotgun in hand. She approached cautiously, stepped over to the rise and looked across the open space. The lion must have bounded down the slope and run, dissolving into the darkness. Cinda was consumed by the thought that what the beast had in its jaws might have been human, or a piece of a human.

Returning to her Explorer, she looked back and saw the hole, then trained her flashlight on it, dirt flung in every direction. She stepped over and beamed her light into the crevice.

Six foot down was a wooden casket that had been ravaged open and was now empty.

Looking around, she saw evidence of the assault. Bones... an arm here, a leg over there; a gnawed ribcage several feet away. What the lion had was human all right, but it was a long-dead human, of no practical use to the beast. The hole was in front of a massive tombstone. Cinda trained her light on the face of it and felt the same chill she'd experienced reading Wolfpaw's letter, especially that one passage, now singed into her memory: *You know Mentex is what I am speaking of. My creature friends are being forced to strike back and strike back harsh.* The name on the tombstone was the same as she'd seen displayed on the imposing statue at the entrance to the Mentex plant. *Elias Howard Lynton, 1820-1881. Father, friend and visionary, who produced the rocks that established our beloved town.*

CHAPTER 12

He never should have made that promise not to kill any of the two-legged humans. Still, he went to the dead place and dug up those ancient bones, sensing that somehow that rotting body had something to do with where they poisoned the water and spit deadly fire into the sky.

Now he would send another message, but not the one he was burning to send. It would not be a human kill, not yet, but it would hurt one of them who helped spread the deadly poison.

He would need to be careful. He'd never attempted something this bold in the daylight. But the world had been turned over; night had become poisonous and remained so through the daylight. And he was not killing for food. There would be no time today for that.

There were around twenty in the pasture. The only one he was interested in was the biggest one, the prize, the white.

Concealed in the cornfield, he crouched, watching the herd as they lazed in the open. He would need to strike before he sparked a stampede, before any of the two-legs could grab their sticks that shot fire.

Now, half the herd was gathered; brown ones, grays, spotted and speckled ones, the white one in the center of it all.

With a mighty push from his back flanks, the lion sprung forward, bounding toward the herd with tremendous speed.

One on the edge glanced over, sensing danger. It snorted, then swung around and awkwardly galloped in the opposite direction. Two others reacted, then three more. To him, these didn't exist; every part of his being was trained on the big white.

And now the white sensed the danger and swung in a half-circle, its eyes having caught the beige blur of the attacker. It lurched first in one direction, then retreated toward the fence. The big white stumbled, rose and was trying to regain its balance when the lion leaped, claws forward, teeth bared as it scraped and tore the pristine coat.

The white fell again, rolling onto its back. It tried to rise but the lion was on its neck, tearing and gnashing, tasting the blood. The white regained its feet and the lion crashed into its side, toppling it, claws thrashing, teeth ripping flesh. A mighty slash of exposed claws tore the underside open. The white tried to rise one final time but some of its insides spilled out, like a wet sack whose bottom had given way. The lion finally reared his head and pushed back.

A torrent of blood was rushing from the white's neck and throat and the light was going out of its eyes, the rest of the herd shrieking and rushing chaotically around.

The lion bounded back across to the cover of the cornfield, fresh blood on his muzzle and snout and paws. He would rush through the high dry stalks, concealed for a time, until he'd need to bound back over the hard ground where things moved even faster than he did. He would keep running to the foot of the mountain, then ascend one of the trails and find cover. He'd rest until nightfall, resisting the nearly overpowering impulse to go back for more tearing that would give him a meal.

Keeping his promise, he had not killed the two-leg who lived there, and needed to be satisfied that he had done what he set out to do; spread out a great blanket of fear.

* * *

Iris, in her riding clothes, was headed out to the pasture to ride Comanche for the very first time. Lowell kept a horse for her private use, a little sorrel named Lady, but Iris had always wanted to ride the white stallion. She smiled to herself, recalling the way she'd gotten Lowell to agree.

Comanche was huge but Iris, raised in Durango, grew up around horses, so she'd have no trouble saddling him once she led him back to the barn. She couldn't wait to get him into a heated gallop. Just looking at the flawless horse was exciting enough, but actually riding him was going to be thrilling.

What did she think about Lowell finally admitting he was married? Iris didn't mind in the least. This thing with Lowell wasn't forever; just a trip through the candy store. He bought her anything she asked for. Besides, she'd been married three times already; the first at sixteen, the longest lasting a year-and-a-half. Marriage was nothing and a girl needed her secrets too.

Iris wasn't really sure whether Lowell owned the place or rented it. When Lowell was lying, he tended to be vague, so it was most likely a rental. The house was okay but the pasture was gorgeous, forty acres of rolling fields.

For Iris, a lot of things were falling into place. She'd made sure that Lowell had set her up as MC for the daytime phase of the Mentex Music Fest, coming up this week-end. Of course, Lowell would be hosting the evening's slate of headliners. But between ten and six Iris would be up there in front of hundreds of people, bringing performers on and off, performing eight numbers of her own throughout the day, backed by a really hot stage band that included teenage guitar prodigy, Barry Quinn.

With all of this swimming in her mind, Iris stopped as though she suddenly realized she was traipsing through a mine field. *What? What the hell?*

Blind with terror, she rushed back toward the house.

* * *

Lowell was at the bar at Ossie's when his cell phone chimed the opening melody of *I'm So Lonesome I Could Cry*. He smiled, knowing it was Iris. "Hello, darlin'." He listened but she wasn't making any sense. "Wait, whoa, hold on, catch your breath. One word at a time now, something's wrong with the herd?" He listened. "Something's wrong with Comanche? Okay, okay, I'll be right there." Before hanging up, he added, "Call the township. Animal Control."

He hurried out to his truck and gunned it all the way to the ranch. He parked beside the barn and Iris came rushing out of the house. "There in the pasture," she uttered.

Lowell strode toward it. As he was opening the gate, he heard Iris's trembling voice behind him. "I can't go out there. I can't go out there again."

The horses were scattered, some lurching in one direction, then another, as though an explosion had been ignited and they were in fear of another blast.

Lowell spotted the white mass, covered with blood and dark matter. Maybe he was still alive. But as he got closer, he knew that was a wishful thought. Comanche, beautiful, powerful, proud Comanche was on his side, a gaping hole ripped in him as though he'd been gutted with a saber. His beautiful dark eyes were open, fixed on some distant point in the mountains.

Lowell sank to his knees and remained frozen for some time. His breath was shallow and he feared he might not totally get it back again. He became aware of a presence behind him. He turned and saw a uniformed female officer.

"Are you all right, Mr. Felker?" Cinda Rigg asked him.

"Yes. No. I don't know." Then, "I just... What did this? What happened? The middle of the day, like this..."

Cinda made a circuit of the carcass, the scene at the graveyard fresh in her mind, then said evenly, "I'd say it was a lion."

Lowell looked up at her like an overgrown child who had just experienced a loss he could not and would never comprehend.

"A lion?" he asked, as though it was a word he'd never heard before.

"I'm afraid so, Mr. Felker," Cinda said, softly.

CHAPTER 13

There was a man-made reservoir just east of the Mentex plant, with beaches for swimming, rafts for the swimmers to relax on, and docks for boating. The water was well-stocked and throughout the summer, you'd see fishermen in rowboats on the smooth, glassy surface.

In the pre-dawn hours, a cloud began forming atop the water, thickening and spreading until the entire reservoir was topped with a fog so dense that, were you in a boat on that water, you couldn't see a foot in front of you.

The fog continued to spread, but only in one direction, west toward the mountains, and by dawn the entire town of Lynton was blanketed.

As though summoned by the fog-bank, they'd started coming down the mountains from north and west of town and from the foothills to the south. They came in silent herds, not rushing, being guided by their leaders. Yet they knew where they were going as they descended, the elders guiding the young ones.

* * *

Todd, who had just rolled out of bed, stood in his kitchen, looked in the bag and noted that there was just enough coffee. He opened the small icebox and realized he'd forgotten to pick up half-and-half. There was milk, but it was low-fat and he'd spoiled himself with the thicker stuff. The grocery wouldn't open until eight but the Wagging Tail commenced business at six.

He threw on some clothes and stepped out onto the front porch. It was getting light but the outdoors was enveloped in a dense fog. He wondered if this was just a pocket or if the whole town was wrapped in it.

He carefully descended the wooden stairs and kept moving

forward. Well, this was different, he thought, having things become visible only as you came right up on them.

Moving slowly, he reached the street and halted, becoming aware of sound and vibration. There was motion too, shapes and blurs before him, beige, mixed with the ghostly, silver-gray fog.

Todd took a careful step forward, then stopped, realizing that he was about to collide into... What? A deer. Another, and another. A whole herd, walking along the road. Todd didn't feel frightened but simply amazed at the bizarre nature of the encounter. Where had they come from, Burnham Park? Where were they going? Deer in Lynton was a usual occurrence. But there were so many. Todd could only make out a shape or two at a time but his impression was that this was a sizeable herd.

He remained standing until it appeared they all had passed. He wasn't needing coffee anymore. He turned to make his way back. The day was starting strangely enough without rushing headlong into it.

* * *

Lowell was behind his desk in his home office, sleep-bleary: draped in a bathrobe, telephone in hand.

"That doesn't make any sense, Claude. If your act can't get here, why the hell should we pay them?" He listened a moment, red-faced and trembling. "Read the contract, partner and you'll see that what we're dealing with here is an act of God." He listened again, taking a fresh glass of coffee from Iris, who'd just come back into the room, wearing nothing but a wet towel folded on top of her head. "Hell no, we haven't determined why the damn things are doing it. I just know that nobody can even—"

The agitated look on Lowell's face turned to stunned anger. He looked over at Iris. "That no-good New York son-of-a-bitch hung up on me."

Iris stood there for a moment. "How many acts have

cancelled?"

"All of the goddamn headliners." He shook his head. "We can't reschedule. I've planned this for months. The whole event's totally fucked."

As Iris left the room, the phone was ringing again. She realized that the look on Lowell's face was one she'd never seen before. World-by-the-balls, got-it-all-handled Lowell Felker had no idea what the hell was going on.

* * *

Todd, alone in his cottage, was watching *Headline News* on the big screen. They kept cycling the top stories and Lynton was third, right behind riots in Seoul and a lockdown of the Milwaukee airport. The female anchor, Todd knew her face but not her name, delivered the story with a curious half-smile.

"Residents of a tiny town remain cut-off from the world. Lynton, Colorado, with two thousand residents, sits at the base of the Rocky Mountains. Denver field reporter Gary Van Dyke is in Lynton... Gary?"

Van Dyke, in shirtsleeves and tie, microphone in hand, filled a tiny box on the top right corner of the screen. He took a couple of seconds for the feed to connect, then jumped in. "If you look behind me, you'll witness civic, county and state authorities trying to determine what to do with literally hundreds of deer that came down from the mountains and, for reasons known only to them, decided to lie down on either end of town, blocking the two roads running in opposite directions that lead into and out of Lynton."

Jennifer, from the left side of the screen, asked, "Are the deer doing anything? Are there any moving around town or are they all simply lying down?"

"As you can see, they're just lying here, taking up at least a city block on each end of the two major streets. If I had to compare it to anything, it's like a peaceful protest, where they're daring the authorities to remove them."

"How long has this been going on, and what are the effects?"

"As I reported earlier, there was a blanket of fog throughout the town this morning. There's been speculation that it somehow disoriented the deer and caused them to leave their accustomed habitat at a higher elevation. But why they'd come down and block traffic like this is anybody's guess."

"How much traffic is affected?"

"This is the main access to Rocky Mountain National Park. And, as this has been going on since dawn, and it's July fourth weekend, traffic is backed up in both directions, affecting things all the way to Denver. Another unfortunate effect is that Lynton hosts a very popular musical festival that has had to be cancelled, not only the acts, but the trucks hauling in the sound and lights, simply don't have access."

Jennifer shook her platinum head. "Well, keep us informed as to any updates."

The remote feed went away, replaced by the anchor smiling once again from her climate-controlled post in Atlanta. "When we come back, we'll find out why some Silicone Valley parents who work in the software industry are encouraging their children to go back to pens and pencils…"

* * *

Iris Avery was on the stage at Ossie's on Sunday evening, fronting a five-piece band. She had on jeans and cowboy boots but the most prominent part of her outfit was a sky-blue blouse with glittering silver sequins all over the front.

Todd had been down at the bar and wandered up, part out of restlessness, part out of curiosity. The instrumentation was Iris on mandolin, supported by bass, fiddle, dobro and a dazzling, fresh-faced guitarist announced as "Barry Quinn, the hottest fourteen-year-old picker in the whole damn country."

The song, a lively kind of swing about having a ball in Birmingham, delivered by Iris in a twang far too pronounced to be natural, ended to vigorous applause. She seemed to have quite a few fans in the house. Todd was surprised that Lowell Felker was not in attendance. It was generally known that Lowell and Iris were involved.

The song ended and Iris beamed as she spoke into the mike. "I wish all ya'all had been able to come out to hear us at Mentex-fest this holiday weekend– that it hadn't gone and got cancelled. Whew, what was that with our deer buddies messin' with our little ole' town? Next time they come down from the mountains like that, I think I'll get me a gun, then cook me up a mess a' venison... We're gonna play you one more before we take us a break. It's a tune I learned me as a girl and it's called Walk Softly on My Heart."

Minutes later, the set concluded, Todd was looking around for the waitress, either to get her to bring the check or to order another beer, he hadn't decided, when Iris appeared at his table: eyes, lips and teeth beaming down on him.

"We haven't met. I'm Iris."

"I know. I... enjoyed you up there. Todd Wendt."

"I know who you are. Lowell's told me all about you."

"You don't say..."

She looked away, as though something had fluttered by. "Well, just that you're from Mentex headquarters."

"Care to sit down?"

Iris took the seat across from him.

"I haven't been able to do much," Todd continued. "It seems like Lowell has his own way of doing things."

"Look, I know Lowell's a control freak, but he's good people."

Todd didn't really know how to respond, had no sense of where this was going.

"Lowell does so much for the folks 'round here and he works

so hard, bless his heart."

"Where's Lowell tonight?" he asked, not knowing what else to say.

"What do you think? He's working. The man never sleeps until he just keels over from exhaustion."

"Working where?"

Iris's breezy demeanor seemed suddenly clouded. "Over at the plant, I guess... Unless he's with Vance, out at the house. That's right, I'm pretty sure that's what he told me. He's workin' at home tonight." She got up suddenly. "I'm gonna go down and clear my head before the next set. A pleasure meeting you. Are you fixin' to stay?"

Todd got up from his chair. "No, I've... got some work of my own."

* * *

Todd walked the half-mile to the plant. No sign of life anywhere. He reached the cyclone-fenced gate at the entrance to Mentex. Although Todd had worked late several nights, he'd never come to work at this hour. In the dim glow, he punched in numbers on the keypad. Vance Dickason had provided him with a five digit entry code. Nothing. He punched the numbers again. Nada. Standing there, he sensed some movement behind and to his left. He turned and saw a guy on either side of forty, head completely shaved, wearing what looked like a dark suede jacket. The guy was big but an even bigger guy stood mutely at his shoulder. What came at Todd was a question, although there was no warmth or friendliness.

"Can I help you with something?"

"I just wanted to do some work tonight. Why isn't the code working?"

"Can I see your employee ID?"

Todd decided to dig in a bit. "Todd Wendt is the name. I can't say I've ever seen you around." He shot a look at the sentry. "You, either."

The guy-in-charge smiled, but again, no warmth, only a kind of malevolent amusement. "Seems like you need to come back in the morning."

"I was told Lowell Felker's here. Why don't you go get him for me?"

Another leer. "Mr. Felker gave direct orders not to be disturbed. And I take my orders from Mr. Felker."

This wasn't going well and it wasn't going anywhere. "What's your name, so I can be clear with Lowell about our conversation tonight?"

The guy now all but grinned. "My name's Cheever. Bart Cheever. You tell Mr. Felker about this and he'll just say I was doing my job."

Todd couldn't see pressing it any further. For one thing, he'd had three pints of Ossie's ale and felt buzzed. Butting heads with these goons, figuratively or literally, was something he shouldn't take on unless he was at the top of his game. He'd make his waves with Felker, first thing in the morning.

He turned and began walking back to town. It was a warm night and the soft lights ahead looked welcoming. He was looking forward to getting home, taking a steaming shower, then hitting the sack. He was on the left side of the highway, walking against any oncoming traffic, when he heard a low sound from behind that kept getting louder. He turned; a pair of headlights were beaming toward him, coming down Highway 64 from the direction of Valmont, the beams high, bright and intense. He squinted and put his hand up to shield his eyes and to see better. This wasn't a car but a truck, a big one. The engine emitted a high wine above its rumble. Todd couldn't recall seeing a truck this big on either of the two-lane highways that led to and from Lynton.

And then something else entered the picture.

A huge bull elk, an expansive rack spread atop its massive body, pushed out of the brush and onto the highway. Its motion was slow and almost purposeful as it stepped onto the pavement, straddling half the road, half-turned toward the oncoming headlights but not reacting in any way. The beams kept coming and Todd watched the bizarre tableau of the enormous elk, with the high and wide cab of the truck bearing down upon it, in frozen fascination.

The instant before the front bumper would have collided with the elk's flank, the truck veered to the right, the sudden change of motion causing it to tip off course and topple to its side. The cab became disengaged and Todd kept looking on in amazement as the elk simply turned in the direction of the mayhem, then loped off the road, bounded over a ditch and disappeared into a set of trees that led to an adjacent field.

Todd walked a few steps, then rushed toward the damaged truck. Only one of the headlights was still beaming. The cab had been pulling a gigantic silver tanker. As Todd was getting up to the scene, a figure was making its way out of the cab from where the front windshield used to be. Todd got closer and saw it was a man, clearly dazed and shaken.

"Are you hurt?" Todd shouted. "Is anybody else in there?"

"What the hell," the guy panted. "Why didn't that thing move?"

Now Todd was right in front of him. "You all right?"

"Yeah, yeah, I'm okay." His hands were shaking as he pulled a pack of cigarettes from his breast pocket.

As he was trying to ignite his lighter, Todd said, "Should you be doing that? There's stuff spilling out of that tanker."

The spark caught and the guy touched the flame to the cigarette's tip. "It's just water. You work at the plant?"

"Yeah," Todd said.

"Then you know. The water gets mixed in up there. If I'd have been coming out rather than going in I wouldn't be lighting up."

He looked around, clearly in disbelief about what he'd just gone through. "Shit, I've been running down here three, four times a night and nothing like this…"

Todd turned and saw Bart Cheever and a couple of guys rushing up. "My God, Lyle, what the hell happened?"

The driver looked around, then back at Cheever. "An elk, man. Biggest one I ever saw. Parked himself right in my lane." He nodded in Todd's direction. "Ask him, he saw it."

Cheever glared at Todd, then turned to the guy beside him. "Put a call in to the town. We need to block this road off."

CHAPTER 14

Todd sat beside Ossie Anderson, high clusters of lights illuminating the twilight in the top row of the bleachers at Burnham Park, watching Ossie's Brewers in a tight match with a team from Parkland.

Ossie spent the early innings explaining to Todd why he was so committed to 'the greatest game ever concocted.' Why he saw it as the team-sport equivalent of chess. Why, due to its zen quality, it was so keenly understood in Japan. Why, because of its poetic nature, it was better on radio than TV. And why, because of the way America had been gutted and leveled and sped up, the future of it was at risk among young people, especially young black people.

"Football and basketball are fine for a fast-paced, televised environment, and you can keep soccer in the suburbs and in South America. But baseball needs to get back to the towns and the neighborhoods."

Todd, preoccupied, nodded in agreement.

"Look at those two umps out there," Ossie was saying. "You got Weatherly on the bases who needs lasik surgery, and that Yablonsky kid behind home plate... barely knows the game. I'll bet he's never heard of the infield fly rule... You're pretty quiet tonight, Todd."

"Sorry, just some problems with work."

It was the bottom of the fifth, three to one, Ossie's Brewers trailing. The visiting pitcher was a tow-headed lanky right-hander with a smoking fastball. There was a runner on first as Barney Crockett, the Brewers' veteran third baseman, stepped up to the left side of the plate. "Okay, let's get something going here," said Ossie. Then he called out, "Pick one you like, Crockett!"

Crockett took the first fastball for a strike, then an outside change-up evened the count.

When he swung from the heels at a belt-high fastball, he missed by half a foot. Ossie cupped his hands around his mouth, then just leaned forward and didn't say anything.

Crockett stepped out of the batter's box, bent down and scooped a handful of dirt which he rubbed on his palms. The next pitch was high and wide but Crockett chased it, his upper body twisted pathetically to end the inning.

"This is turning ugly," Ossie said, as he rose off his seat. "The snow cone truck just pulled up. You want me to bring you back one?"

"No thanks," said Todd.

It was fully dark now: the glowing lights, the green field, the brown base paths. Todd's eye was caught by something near the branches of a nearby tree... a trio of bats, fluttering and swirling. He glanced around. No one else seemed to be taking notice of them. He looked back and one of the bats veered and swooped toward the bleachers and, although it was high, Todd felt himself all but duck in response.

He laughed to himself but it was a tight, nervous laugh. He looked up and the bats were still fluttering. They appeared to be facing him, kind of treading air. Then, as though some kind of signal had bounced among the three of them, the bats veered off like they were fleeing the artificial lights before dissolving into the blue-black sky.

* * *

While she had previously enjoyed the all-night shift, Officer Cinda Rigg was dreading it. Before, she'd found her circuits of the town to be meditative and soothing. Her night shift began at ten and she was effectively on her own, like a cab driver trolling for nocturnal fares. She knew the job well, what was expected of her and what she could anticipate. But the coyote taunting of Todd Wendt, the ravaged grave of Elias Howard Lynton and the vicious and lethal assault on Lowell Felker's beautiful white stallion made her fear what had once been benign. And deer coming down from the mountains and blocking the town was beyond unusual. She felt she was in foreign and hostile territory, some fairy tale kid lost in the deep dark woods. Wolfpaw's warning was etched in her brain. And what about Wolfpaw – where had he gone? She wished she could talk with him to see if he would be able or willing to shed further light on what she now regarded as a perilous situation.

She pulled out of the station a little after ten and found herself cautious where she had once been carefree: anxious where she'd once been at ease. She remembered a film she'd seen about some men who were driving a pair of trucks loaded with nitro-glycerin through the rain forest. The terrain was anything but friendly and they could incinerate at any second. Cinda now had a heightened awareness about every sound and sensation. Her palms were damp; her mouth was dry, with queasiness in her chest and gut. She was driving slower than usual, twenty or twenty-five, well under the forty miles per hour she often maintained while cruising South Center Street.

The town appeared haunted. She kept imagining the rough scene it had been in the 1800s and tried to picture what it might look like a hundred years from this night. She could imagine it in the past but not the future. Cinda felt that right then, that moment, the community was locked in some silent struggle that could doom it forever, and could not conceive of what it would be like even six months ahead. The people who lived here would keep going about their business, distracted by their day-to-day lives, until they could ignore things no longer and what was now silently oppressing the town was creeping through their windows and busting into their houses.

Cinda had turned and was gliding past the middle school playground. Again, she thought of a filmed image, this one from the 1950s, of kids ducking under their wooden desks and tables as though doing so would shield them from the effects of a nuclear blast. To her, the houses she passed looked abandoned or shut up in some kind of flimsy defense. The trees had faces, their branches were arms reaching out, not to embrace her but to pull her closer, squeezing until she could no longer breathe. The bushes would encircle her legs and once they'd ensnared her, would force her to the ground.

She was at the cemetery now, white pillars at its entrance. Above was a top border, also white, with shapes that jutted downward. Those pale shapes now struck Cinda as a set of upper teeth, leering at her. She realized she had pressed down on the brake and her Ford Explorer was halted at the entrance. She'd been reluctant before to go inside but now she was petrified. It was some kind of challenge she knew, but who else was going to know that now, this night, these moments, she simply couldn't summon the courage to go further?

She spent the next hour-and-a-half, cruising the familiar streets, silently berating herself for not driving into the graveyard. Around midnight, she decided she would drive out Highway 64 towards Valmont, then along some of the back roads that bordered the farms and ranches. It would be good for her, she thought, to drive by Lowell Felker's spread, and try to neutralize the revulsion she was feeling from the sight of his gorgeous stallion reduced to ribbons.

Cinda's Explorer was approaching the bridge that spanned above the highway when she took her foot off the gas. A black shape was blocking the center of her lane. Her first thought was that a cow or a bull had escaped from of one of the nearby pastures. Pressing the brake, she realized there was another black shape near it, this one in the foreground and more in the middle of the road. She flicked the brights and her headlights played off both objects, so black they appeared radiant. She was maybe twenty yards away when they began moving, their motion strange and seemingly awkward, although surprisingly fast. They didn't move like cattle and, as she bore down on them, realized what she was seeing were a pair of black bears, bounding to her left, away from the bridge that, once it spanned the highway, led into Mentex.

Cinda veered right, bringing her Explorer to a halt on the side of the road closest to the plant. She breathed deeply. She'd seen bears, of course, but never two together. And she felt she'd come up on them when they were in the midst of something, that their proximity to Mentex was purposeful.

As she sat behind the wheel, she looked to her left. The bears had scurried across the field beyond the opposite side of the highway, swallowed up by the greenery and the night. The trees and bushes, the rocks and hills were somehow closer, and it was anything but a soothing feeling. And then it hit her…

Two bears… It was two bears that had slaughtered everyone at Ned Haddock's house.

That's why there was blood leading from the house and why there were tracks leading up to the driveway. One bear had been inside, mauling Ned and his son. The other had been outside and attacked Jessica Rafferty as she ran terrified from the house.

As Cinda eased the Explorer into first, it was like she was no longer driving, but instead, being driven. The Explorer made a U-turn and glided for about a mile until it eased over to the left, pulling up alongside a one-story wooden structure with a set of neon signs that said *Coors, Bud Light, Corona.* An open widow glowed beneath a red sign that said *Drive-up.*

A scrawny, t-shirted boy slouched on the other side. He looked too young to drink, let alone to be tending a liquor store. If the kid was thrown by having a police cruiser appear at the window, he certainly didn't appear so. Nor did he seem at all surprised when Cinda asked for a pint of Smirnoff.

After she'd given him the cash, the kid shoved the bottle in a paper bag and held it out through the window. Cinda reached for it but her arm froze halfway. The last time she'd drank, she'd woken up on the sofa to find broken glass all over the hardwood floor. Ryland had been with his father for the weekend and Cinda remembered frantically sweeping and vacuuming, fearing that she'd miss a shard and Ry would cut his foot once he was back home.

Cinda threw the Explorer into drive, pushed down on the accelerator and left the kid in the drive-up window literally holding the bottle. As she pulled away, she heard, "Hey, officer. Don't you want your money back?"

* * *

Todd was seated on a bench in Juniper Park, waiting for Officer Rigg. She had left a note on the porch that morning, saying she needed to see him. They agreed to meet in an hour. He'd arrived ten minutes early, was mildly enjoying the towering mountains to the west and the open space before him, soothed by the lively sounds of a half-dozen children on the playground across the way.

She arrived in her white SUV and Todd watched her get out. Having been too distressed when she'd rescued him from the pack of coyotes, he now had the opportunity to really look at her. She wasn't tall, five three or four, with chin-length blonde hair that was black at the roots. In uniform, she filled a pair of boots that were practically knee high. She was not slight, nor was she heavy. Her gait projected strength and purpose, stating that she was physically in command of herself. Todd considered rising as she got closer, then stayed as he was.

"Thanks for being punctual," she said with a smile.

Todd met her smile with one of his own. "When a police officer calls a meeting, it's best to be on time."

She sat down across from him. "It wasn't really an official request."

"No?" said Todd.

Cinda seemed to not know how to begin, green eyes glistening with an emotion that Todd couldn't discern: sorrow, frustration? The wind was blowing warm against his cheek.

"You're going to have to excuse me," she said. "I didn't sleep last night."

Some kind of inane response rose up in Todd's throat and he let it stay there.

Cinda turned to him. "Have you ever come across something you simply couldn't explain?"

"How do you mean?"

"What if I told you that what happened with those coyotes…" She shook her head as though trying to release a distressing thought. Then she came out with it. "I have a feeling it wasn't random. That you were… targeted."

Todd felt a wave of uneasiness pass through him.

Cinda went on, choosing her words with care. "There was something systematic in the way they were taunting you. And now I feel… and I know this seems insane… but I feel that somehow the fact that you came here to work with Mentex might have made you the object of… interest, to those creatures."

Todd looked once again at the mountains, his eyes roving their brown sand and green trees and red stone faces. Although he could see nothing stirring, those earth sculptures were teeming with life, suggesting worlds which, especially at this moment, seemed truly foreign.

PART TWO

STRANGE THINGS HAPPENING

CHAPTER 15

The Lynton Town Hall was a low, wooden, one-story structure in need of painting. Court proceedings were held there, usually traffic violations, disorderly conduct and domestic incidents. Tonight was a town meeting with twice as many citizens as were usually in attendance. A vote would be taken to choose a mayor who would serve until November's general election. Thus far, those present whose names had been put forth had immediately begged off.

"I nominate Verna Stickley," a male voice called out. "She doesn't like meetings, but she has some good ideas about what to do with those potholes over on Third. My truck had to be aligned because of them and I know Verna's committed to getting them taken care of."

"She's not here," said Beverly Walsh, who was chairing the meeting. "In a special circumstances election, which is what we're having, any nominated candidate needs to be present. If Verna was interested, she'd have come."

"I nominate Ed Gartenhausen," said a woman. "You studied accounting, didn't you, Ed?"

"Statistics," Ed told those assembled. "But only for a year and I didn't get a degree."

"I nominate Lowell Felker." All eyes turned to the aisle seat where Vance Dickerson, in a black, embroidered shirt and black slacks and boots was seated. Although only a few at the meeting knew who he was, they all knew Lowell, either respecting or resenting him. He was seated beside Vance, wearing a bolo tie, cowboy boots, and a smirk on his broad, ruddy face.

This was a surprise nomination and one that needed to be taken seriously.

Ossie Anderson stood up and said, "All due respect, Lowell. Don't you have enough on your plate?"

Lowell turned and glanced at Ossie, but then was clearly addressing the entire hall. "I see it as my civic responsibility. I worked real close with former Mayor Haddock, so I'm already up to speed on the workings of the town. We're not talking rocket science. And what I can't figure out, I'll do like I do at the plant. Delegate."

A few people chuckled but the room was unsettled.

Beverly Walsh scanned the crowd for further nominations when a voice boomed from the back of the hall.

"What about the water, Mr. Felker?"

All eyes turned to Dale Wiggins, who owned Spokes, the bicycle shop on North Center Street. In his late-forties, atop his tight, sinewy frame was a stubble covered face, an untamed head of graying hair, and round, thick-lensed glasses perpetually in need of cleaning. From April to October, no one saw him in anything but a t-shirt, invariably a memento from some rock concert several years back, cut-off jeans and dilapidated sandals.

"Am I the only one whose tap water's been tasting like somebody took a leak in it?" He looked straight across at Lowell Felker. "It's been that way ever since that explosion at the plant last spring."

A tense moment, then Beverly said, "Are you nominating yourself, Dale; is that where this is leading?"

"No, I'm just trying to—"

"I'll nominate him," a male voice called out. "My water's been tasting funny, too."

"I second the nomination" said Ed Gartenhausen. "Dale Wiggins, for mayor of Lynton."

"*Interim* mayor," corrected Beverly. "Any further nominations?"

"Hold on a second," said Dale, clearly flustered, "that's not what I—"

Cinda Rigg, in uniform, shouted out in her New Zealand accent. "I move that the nominations be closed."

Lowell turned in his seat and looked at Cinda as she stood in the back of the hall. "Are you even a citizen, ma'am?" he drawled. "Can you even vote?"

Ossie Anderson called out. "I've read the by-laws, Lowell. They don't say anything about needing to be a registered voter to make a motion."

Lowell turned back around and addressed the front of the hall. "All right, let's get on with it."

* * *

The meeting over, Dale Wiggins was outside the Town Hall, bent over his road bike, opening the lock. Sensing someone behind him, he turned to see Lowell Felker.

"I just come over to congratulate you," said Lowell, thrusting his hand forward.

Dale looked down as though trying to determine if the gesture was authentic, then rather reluctantly offered his own hand.

"No hard feelings is what I'm saying," Lowell continued. "The way I see it, we'll be working together anyway."

"Oh really, how you figure?"

"C'mon, Dale. Mentex is the only real game in town. As goes Mentex, so goes Lynton."

The guy was audacious, you had to hand it to him. Dale smiled. "I guess we'll see about that."

"You've got an open invitation to come by the plant for a stem-to-stern tour. You ever been inside our facility?"

Dale shook his head.

"Well, come on and see for yourself. You'll find I run me a tight ship, clean as a whistle. Whatever boom you think you heard that night came from someplace else. Our plant shuts down at five p.m. sharp, Monday through Friday."

As Dale mounted his road bike, he was thinking, *what have I gotten myself into?* Still, he was pleased. He'd always followed politics and had a sense he could do things better than they were getting done, although a real run for office was something he'd never wanted to expose himself to. He was fine to just run his shop, smoke his weed and remain under the radar.

His route home was east, down South Center Street. The bike lane ran right alongside the traffic and his bike was well lit front and back so he pedaled at a swift clip. The two channels of Center Street merged into the two-lane road that ran into and out of town, and he was nearing his place in no time.

He would call Lydia as soon as he got home. Well, as soon as he got home and lit up a blunt. God bless Colorado, he could hardly believe they made pot legal. He wondered how hard she'd laugh when he told her he'd just become mayor of Linton. They'd been living apart for what, a year now? Five years together and one day she said, "I want to spend more time in Boulder, it's much closer to work." Next thing Dale knew he was helping her pack boxes into her jeep. They still talked every day, often more than once, and when she came out to Lynton every other week or so, she'd usually spend the night.

He passed the hardware store and was approaching the glaring lights of the Pump It Up service station, there was no immediate traffic coming or going. From the corner of his eye he caught a blur to his right and his head involuntarily turned. In the white glare, the blur took shape and picked up speed and, as it flashed by, Dale saw it was a large, rust-shaded fox with white ears and a white tail.

Wow, it must have been running right alongside him to have cut so close like that. He'd seen them before, but almost always from a distance. Now it was bounding along directly in front of Dale's bike. *What's the hell does it think it's doing?* What looked to be a huge semi was approaching in the opposite lane, maybe a hundred yards away. Dale sensed some motion on his right and glanced down to see another fox, also red, keeping pace with him. This fox veered toward him and took a nip at Dale's ankle. It was all Dale could do to keep the handlebars steady.

The lights from the semi were getting closer. The second fox took another nip and this time tore a bit of skin from Dale's ankle. Dale cried out as much in surprise as in pain, although the wound stung immediately.

The fox who'd attacked him swung away. Once the semi passed, Dale would turn left and cross the road to his place. He wondered how deep the bite was, whether he'd need to go to the emergency room in Boulder. He hoped he had some Neosporin in the medicine cabinet. He kept buying the stuff and then misplacing it. Dale sensed some other movement down and to the right and this time a fox whose sleek coat was dark gray was keeping pace with him. The semi was almost upon him, still filling its lane, but this strange dark creature appeared to be nipping the front tire. But then Dale saw that no, there was something filling its mouth. It was thick and pale and looked to be a slab of wood protruding from either side of the fox's jaws. The fox swung its head as though shaking something off but then released the slab, flinging it with a vigorous shake of its head and then this branch, this stick, whatever the hell it was sailed into the wheel, tangling the spokes. Dale was flung over the handlebars, fortunate to be wearing a helmet as the side of his head crashed into the pavement and he rolled to the left.

He lay there stunned, wanting to rise to his feet but knowing he needed to clear his head. What was that sound? It was high and keening and then there was a blare, like a thunderous explosion and he looked up and the lights were bearing down on him, the semi getting closer, not swerving to avoid him. The front wheels on the left of the massive cab were about to crush him when Dale rolled further left, turning completely over until he lay on his back on the warm, harsh pavement. He felt the whoosh and rumble as the massive cab and van passed over him.

Lying in the open like a man who'd just fallen from a great height, Dale tried to assess the damage. He was alive but it had been close. From beyond him, up ahead, the brake lights of the semi glowed red as blood while the van pulled over to a stop.

What had happened? A fox, three foxes, had all but run him into the semi. Where the hell were they anyway? Dale pushed up from both elbows and glanced over to the side of the road. The biggest fox Dale had ever seen was staring at him, eyes burning through the darkness. Wait, no, it was not a fox but a coyote. Dale locked eyes with it for a moment, feeling as though the animal might rush forward and attack him while he was down. But the coyote appeared to nod in some kind of silent affirmation, then bound away, leaving Lynton's new mayor stunned and shaken.

CHAPTER 16

On his desktop computer, Todd typed *Confidential* in the e-mail heading, reminding himself there was never any guarantee that a message would not be forwarded. But Sandoval was the one who'd sent him to Lynton, so he figured the head of the company was invested in Todd's time being well-spent.

Todd wrote that he felt shut out by Lowell Felker, and would have to start stepping on toes if he were to make any real headway.

Sandoval got back to him immediately: *You are totally supported here at headquarters. Take any measures you feel are necessary to preserve and promote the interests of Mentex-Colorado. I am leaving tonight on a three week cruise and look forward to a complete update upon my return.*

Todd called Edna to his office, then asked her to close the door.

"I need a copy of the operational budget," he told her. "Can you get it for me?"

"That's finance, Sarah Haddington's department. We have a good relationship but I'm not sure she'd just hand it over."

"Tell her the request is coming from Herman Sandoval. If she drags her feet, I have documentation to back it up."

* * *

When Todd stepped into Lowell's office, Lowell looked up from his desk, tiny eyes squinting as though gazing at something far in the distance.

"You've been a hard man to find these past couple of days," said Todd.

"It doesn't all get done here in the office, Wendt. I've been working out in the field, like I thought you'd be doing. I heard you were here to witness that truck going off the road because of some dumb-ass elk. Sometimes we take for granted all the beasts that are roaming around these parts."

"We all got off lucky. The driver missed him by an inch."

"If you need to come in at night, let me know ahead of time. We've been changing the code regularly due to security concerns."

"What kind of work were you doing here on a Sunday night?"

"Cleaning out the kilns. We want to make sure we're running as clean as possible, well beyond EPA standards." He winked. "Gotta keep everybody happy."

"There were some extra bodies on hand. That security guy, Bart Cheever. Why doesn't his name show up on the human resources roster?"

"He's not here on a regular basis. Now what can I do for you?"

"I've been going over the operational budget..."

Lowell jerked involuntarily. "Who gave it to you?"

"I have permission from Sandoval himself. If you'd like to see it, I have an e-mail to that effect."

"Why are you bothering with the budget? That's not part of your job description."

Todd glanced down at the paper. "According to this we're currently short over one hundred eighty-five thousand dollars. I need to see how and where those funds have been applied."

Lowell stood and glared at him. "Look, Wendt, I've been running this plant for seven years. Our new budget became effective on July first. Things come up throughout the year that are unanticipated. To make up for overages the previous fiscal year, yes, I sometimes have to dip into the new budget to catch up, which is exactly what I did."

"You cleared this with headquarters?"

Lowell's face was turning red. "Sandoval fills my coffers every July and I spend it accordingly. There's never been any complaint from headquarters about the way I run the ship here."

"Where are the line items for those funds, Lowell? I'd like to see—"

"Tell you what, friend. I'll call Mex-City by the end of today and set up a three-way with Sandoval, so we can get ourselves a really clear picture of what you can and can't stick your nose into around here."

* * *

In the conference room of Angie's office, Ginger Kincaid sat at the long table, hands folded, looking apprehensive. She'd dressed up, as Angie had instructed, in a matching blouse and skirt.

Angie herself was dressed more casually in a pants suit, and Clive, her young, male, paralegal, sat with his fingers on the keys of his laptop. Although this was just a dress rehearsal, Angie's tone and manner were all business. "We are in the law offices of Angela Prez to take the deposition of Ginger Louise Kincaid of Lynton, Colorado, concerning the circumstances of the death of her late husband, Francis Reese Kincaid, also of Lynton, who was, at the time of his death, employed by Mentex International." She looked at Ginger. "Are you all set, you want some more water or anything?"

"No, I'm fine, thank you." Ginger shifted a bit in her chair, which appeared too big for her.

"Let's go right to the morning of your husband's death. Your testimony is that Frank was working an all-night shift at Mentex's Lynton facility, is that correct?"

"That's right."

"And what were his duties at Mentex?"

"His duties?"

"How would you characterize his role there?"

"Well, Frank did whatever they told him to do, I guess.

Labor, you know. He also, because he'd been there a while, got to supervise some of the crews he was assigned to. A foreman, he called it."

"That was a formal title?"

"I don't know. It seemed like it was."

"And what were his duties the night before he died?"

Ginger shifted herself again. "I don't really know."

"Was it unusual for him to be working all night?"

"Yes and no. They'd stepped up production."

"Cement production?"

"I suppose it was. That's what they make there."

"Did your late husband ever allude to some new project that Mentex had taken on? One that not everybody at Mentex was privy to?"

Ginger took a moment. "If he ever did, I'm not sure how seriously I would have taken it. Frank liked to talk big sometimes. Make things seem bigger than what they really were."

"Let's turn back for a moment to that morning – that terrible morning, when Frank collapsed and died at home. Where were you when it happened?"

"I don't know exactly when it happened. I came home and found him."

"Came home from where?"

Ginger looked vaguely startled. "What's the question?"

"Where were you coming from that morning when you discovered Frank's body?"

Ginger studied her small, pale hands. She looked like she was about to burst into tears. "I took the kids to school. It was my day to drive the car pool. Then, instead of coming home, I think I went to the Wagging Tail and had a coffee."

"You *think* you did?"

"I'm pretty sure. I've blocked out a lot of details. It's all still pretty traumatic."

"If you did, in fact, go there, did you pay with cash or a credit card?"

"A debit card, probably. Why is that important?"

"If you paid with a debit card, then there's a record of the transaction... Who else is in your car pool?"

Again, Ginger looked startled. "Why is *that* important?"

Angie broke character again. "Ginger, if you testify that you were driving a car pool and that was why you weren't there to possibly assist your husband, the defense will want to substantiate that. They'll want to know every single detail; that's why it's so vital that we're doing this before going forward."

There was a long moment. Angie looked over at Clive who still had his fingers poised on the keys.

Ginger rose out of her chair. On her way out the door she said, without turning around. "There's no way I can do this. No way in hell."

Angie felt the air go out of her. The room was quiet for a long stretch of time. Finally, Clive leaned back and looked at Angie. "Guess she's not ready."

"No," said Angie with a look on her face that was both far away and consumed by the moment. Once the sound of Ginger's heels faded, Angie added, "And I'd love to find out why the woman is lying her ass off."

CHAPTER 17

At Mentex, practically the only person Todd interacted with was Edna, his assistant, but she possessed no knowledge of the inner-workings of the plant. Lowell Felker had clearly put the word out. The man had carved out a little fiefdom and was either feared or adored, or both, by those with whom he surrounded himself. Vance Dickason was his most consistent buffer, coming around Todd's office in what Todd interpreted as a kind of genial surveillance. Whatever Todd was going to accomplish here, would need to be done on his own.

The bronze Chevrolet Malibu that Mentex had provided sat under the carport for days after its delivery. Todd remained in town and walked wherever he wanted or needed to go. There was no postal delivery in Lynton. Every residence or business was assigned a PO box and you had to go in yourself and pick up your mail. Todd initially thought this would serve as a kind of quaint ritual; breeze in every other day or so and enjoy a pleasant exchange with the postal clerk while you collected your correspondence. Like many things in Lynton, it didn't work out that way. The woman who lorded over the post office, Helen was her name, made nearly every interaction strained and unpleasant. There were two types of post office box: a small one and a somewhat larger one. Anyone getting a box for the first time had to settle for a smaller one, even if a larger one were available. You needed to claim your mail within ten business days. After that, any mail that had accumulated in the box, plus any being held would be sent back without an explanation. Todd wasn't even sure if that were legal.

Such intractability was not confined to the post office. The liquor store in the main part of town was owned by a guy who would demand a picture ID for every transaction. During the third encounter, Todd asked, "Isn't the credit card enough?"

The guy looked up balefully. "Ever heard of identity theft, mister?"

Todd vowed never to step in there again.

His first trip to the local library included looking for an author whose new book had been reviewed in the *Sunday Times*. "We don't have any of her work," was the male librarian's terse reply.

"Can you order it?" Todd asked.

"I'm afraid not. I went to one of her signings and she wasn't very friendly."

"And for that the public library won't order her books?"

Not everyone in town was like this, but enough so that you had to choose your interactions. The other frustration was that, due to the limited in-town choices, the Lynton merchants tended to gouge their customers. The drugstore, the copy place, the ice cream parlor, the lone gourmet restaurant, all ran prices a third above what one would pay in Valmont or even in Boulder.

He'd sampled the few restaurants in town and found himself pretty consistently at Ossie's Blues n' Brew, most often seated at the bar, talking with Ossie. They had settled into a mutual familiarity that Todd enjoyed. He got to know even more about Ossie by tuning into his Saturday night radio show, *Night Tracks*. During the show, which ran midnight to three, Ossie programmed blues and jazz and featured the upcoming attractions at his club, which necessitated him including bluegrass and folk along with the other music. Beamed out of a rented shack across from the library, the signal was weak but it was streamed and archived on the internet, so anybody who didn't live in range could tune in at their leisure. Ossie also talked about his Brewers, the game they'd just won or lost, and the game or games slated for the week, urging local listeners to come out and support them.

After yet another day of combing through files and perusing web sites, the most interesting thing Todd came across was that Lowell Felker, five years before, had begun melting down discarded tires as a fuel source. *"Tires produce the same energy*

as petroleum and 25 percent more energy than coal," Lowell stated.
*"The only way to dispose of scrap tires is to burn them, so thousands
of tires are just sitting there, waiting to be accessed."*

A clip from the Boulder Daily Observer quoted Angie Prez of
the Colorado Earth Angels *"Atmospheric contamination drastically
increases when tire rubber is incinerated for fuel. Allowing Mentex to
burn tires would set a horrendous precedent."*

The EPA authorized its own emergency study, concluding
that: *"During the combustion process (with complete combustion being
reached at 1202 degrees Fahrenheit) Polychlorinated dibenzodioxins
and furans are produced. Dioxins (PCDDs) have been established as
substantial environmental pollutants, dating back to the Industrial
Revolution of the 1800s. Furans are highly toxic and could be
carcinogenic."* It went on to say *"Members of the PCDD family bio-
accumulate in humans and wildlife due to their lipophilic properties.
When this occurs, there has been strong evidence of developmental
disturbances including respiratory disease and cancer."*

In the wake of such widespread outrage, Lynton's mayor,
Ned Haddock, had agreed with the county when they rescinded
permission to burn tires. Lowell Felker's response appeared in
The Observer. *"The government's report is biased and disappointing.
The energy stored in those tires should be put to good use rather than
rotting in a landfill somewhere."*

Since then, Mentex-Lynton had apparently engaged in nothing
outside the established practices related to the manufacturing
of cement. Under Felker's management, the plant seemed to
have done everything it could to bridge community relations
in Lynton and all of Boulder County. What resistance they
encountered was purely ideological and there wasn't much to
be done about it short of leaving Lynton, with no assurance that
such resentment would not be present somewhere else.

Done for the day, Todd stepped out into the balmy evening
and walked west to Highway 38, a stretch that was becoming
familiar. He could mark his progress in any number of ways,

one being that the closer he got to town the more the speed
limit dropped: from fifty-five to forty, then forty to twenty-five.
The highway transformed to North Center Street and he knew
that going straight back to his place meant another evening of
leftovers and Direct TV. All week, Todd had felt like kicking
himself. While talking with Felker, why hadn't he remembered
that Sandoval was on a ship somewhere and was unavailable?
What troubled Todd was whether Lowell knew that, and his
seeming willingness to contact Sandoval was a stall for time.

It had occurred to him to check the company's weekly online
newsletter that went out to all plants and employees all over the
globe. There it was on page one: *Herman Sandoval to Take Well
Deserved Cruise.* Clearly, Lowell had already seen the newsletter
or, at any rate, knew damn well that the boss couldn't be reached.

With nothing to be done until Sandoval's return, Todd kept
his distance from Lowell.

At the post office, he found that his box was packed with
the usual bills and junk mail. Among them was a stark white
envelope with his name, box and zip code and no return address.

Todd stepped over to a mini-counter and opened it. Typed on
plain white paper: *If you want your Mentex questions answered, be
at Rudy's on Highway 64 Thursday at 10 p.m.*

Todd stared at the message. Part of him wanted to rip it up
and throw it out but part of him was intrigued. By the time he
crossed the post office parking lot and walked to where the blue
neon of Ossie's was glowing up ahead, he'd already made his
decision.

* * *

As Todd entered Ossie's, he headed for the dining room. There
were eight booths and as many tables, about three-quarters of
the room occupied. The chalkboard announced it was *All-You-
Can-Eat Gumbo Night!* Todd was fine with beans but he'd crossed

sausage off his menu long ago. He decided he'd order fish and chips, perhaps substituting something healthier for the second part of the equation. What he really wanted was an Ebony Ale; surely two, maybe three, depending on whether Ossie was around to chat.

Scanning the room for a table, Todd's eyes fell upon Ossie in a booth in the far corner, facing the entrance. He spotted Todd and motioned for him to come over.

As Todd got closer, he noted that he'd never seen Ossie sitting in the dining room before. In fact, he'd rarely seen him sitting, but rather on his feet behind or around the bar, in more or less constant motion.

Todd reached the table and saw that Ossie had a glass of water in front of him. The black-haired woman seated across from him had finished dinner, an empty bowl and cleaned plate in front of her.

"Are you up for some music tonight?" Ossie asked Todd.

"No, I just thought I'd grab a bite."

"I'm putting on Dynamite Candy, a band from Seattle who's making their way back west. For white boys, they actually seem to know a bit about the blues. I'll waive the cover for you."

"Thanks, I'll see how I feel after I eat."

Ossie's companion was looking up at Todd with an engaging smile.

"Todd Wendt, this here's an old... no, make that a long-time friend, Angie Prez."

She graciously held out her hand and Todd shook it, saying, "Oh, I just came across your name."

Angie's smile faded slightly, a quizzical look replacing it. "Where would that have been?"

Todd paused, knowing he'd waded into some water without checking the temperature. "Actually, I was reviewing your web page, the Colorado Earth Angels."

"Todd here just got to town," said Ossie, catching on and

trying to be helpful.

"Oh," said Angie. "What brings you here?"

"I work for Mentex."

Angie gave him the kind of look that an ex-lover from a badly ended relationship might have at an unexpected encounter. "You must be the PR gun that Mentex has brought in to try and calm down the natives."

"That isn't exactly how I'd put it."

"Maybe in your next communique you can let the community know what kind of new poison you've been cooking up." Angie shot Ossie a how could you look.

Ossie lifted his hands in a gesture of helplessness. "Didn't mean to ruin anybody's evening. Both of you are friends of mine and I'm just Switzerland." Sliding out of the booth, he said, "I'm gonna go see if that band needs anything before their set starts."

Todd remained standing as Angie pushed out of her seat. Breezing by him, and it was a chilly breeze, she uttered, "Unfortunately, I'm sure we'll be seeing each other again."

* * *

Angie had come to Ossie's Blues n' Brew that evening with a purpose. Even though she'd all but given up on Ginger, Angie was determined to find out what the woman knew. Angie had one solid source inside the plant named Harold Billings for whom she'd gotten a big settlement for a motorcycle accident. Billings was well aware of Angie's crusade against Mentex and he despised his bosses, Lowell Felker in particular. Yet when she called him, Billings knew nothing about any overnight production. As for Frank Kincaid, he said that Angie should talk to Frank's brother, Kent.

"I remember him from the funeral," she'd said. "Does he work at the plant?"

"Naw," Billings told her, "he's at the body repair shop. Most nights, Kent's at the bar at Ossie's. He doesn't seem to know many people in town, moved here from Nebraska about a year ago. Took his brother's death pretty hard. Frank might have told him something that could help you out."

Sure enough, Kent Kincaid was perched on a stool when Angie entered the bar.

Billings had described the man down to the camouflage cap he usually wore. Angie took the barstool beside Kent. After ordering an ebony ale, she said, "Aren't you Kent Kincaid, Frank Kincaid's brother?"

Kent looked at her. He'd had more than a few and his eyes reflected it. "What if I am?"

Angie put her hand out. "Angie Prez. I'm very sorry about Frank. In fact, I'm looking into the case to see if there's any responsibility on the part of Mentex."

Kent realigned his weight on the barstool. "Ginger told me about you... We talk a lot," he added.

"Can you help me get clear on a few things?"

Kent didn't indicate that he could or he couldn't, so Angie pressed on.

"I'm trying to recreate the timeline of that morning. After Frank came home and was apparently in difficulty, he called your cell."

"Who says he did?"

"I've seen the phone records."

Kent looked down at his empty glass. "I never knew he called till later. Look, Miss. Perez—"

"Prez. Angie Prez."

"I know you mean to go after Mentex, whether it's Frank's case or something else, but you're just upsetting people."

"What people?" asked Angie.

"Well, me for one. And Ginger. Everybody needs time to, you know, get used to Frank being gone."

"Too bad Ginger can't recall where she was when Frank died.

If she could, she'd be more of a help."

"She was driving the kids to school that morning."

"I talked to the other families in the car pool. It was a Monday and Ginger only drove one morning a week, Friday."

Kent turned and faced her. "Look, lady. I don't know what you're up to, but it almost seems like you're accusing Ginger of something. Ginger's a fine woman. When I told her Frank had died, she just went to pieces. Couldn't talk for hours. I had to help pull her together so she could be there for the kids."

"That's odd. In Ginger's statement, she said she came home and found Frank's body. Now you're telling me that you're the one who found him?"

Kent got off his barstool, went to one at the end of the bar, sat down, and ordered another drink.

CHAPTER 18

Around eleven, Todd was up in his loft, in bed but not asleep. The altitude was affecting him, drying him out. He went downstairs and drank two glasses of water. Feeling warm, he considered turning on the air, then cracked a window and flicked on the flat-screen television. The first image he saw was tornado damage in Kansas. He flipped to highlights of the World Cup, then to that cop show that was always on, with a scene of a New York street. He kept flipping. A woman on a talk-show was pouring something over some guy's head... An alligator, emerging from a swamp... The aftermath of a helicopter crash... He switched it off, then stretched out on the sofa.

He lay in the dark, the river rushing beyond the open window. The digital clock on the stove told him it was 11:13. He hadn't slept well since Rene died, waking usually two or three times throughout the night. Sometimes he would read or listen to the radio, or even turn on his computer and work or waste time.

He lay there, playing re-wind, a game he'd invented years before, where he would picture an event from the month he was living in, then the previous month, then the month before that. He tried not to recall the same images each time. One time he got all the way back to seventh grade. Tonight he was vaguely conjuring last summer, July, but now sleep was drifting over him; down, down and then it was dark and peaceful and he knew he'd be good for a few hours anyway.

* * *

Todd felt an odd weight on his chest. Something told him to respond slowly or to not respond at all. Was he dreaming? He glanced at the digital clock. The glowing red numerals said 3:31. He moved his right arm, lifting it carefully. As he eased it toward his chest its progress was interrupted by something solid and... hairy... covered with hair. It was dark in the room but there were shadows from the moonlight coming through the window. He lifted his head, then saw a massive form on his chest. Its face looked milky-pale with black eyes staring at him. The effect of those eyes was somehow mesmerizing. Todd gazed back at them. Time either stood still or had accelerated.

He was now awake and this was real. He drew his right arm back and swung with all his strength. The thing toppled to Todd's left, then in a frantic, continuous motion, as though a button had been pushed and its image drastically speeded up, sprang off the sofa and onto the hardwood floor. Todd shot to his feet, never taking his eyes off the creature as it bounded to the windowsill, rose on its hind legs and pulled itself up and out the open widow.

Todd was breathing hard: disoriented, heart pounding. He rushed across the room and peering out saw the thing loping away through the tight grassy area beside his place.

A possum.

Huge and pale, like the biggest rat he ever could have imagined, had been in his home, on his chest. Todd slammed the window closed, then paced for a moment, heart racing.

He got in the shower and scrubbed, especially his chest, until his skin felt raw. A possum, a *fucking possum* had crawled in, then parked itself on his bare chest.

Curled upstairs in bed, Todd wondered if he'd ever sleep again.

* * *

Ginger was sitting on her back porch. She had spent many hours there, especially since Frank's death. Ginger didn't know what time it was but felt pretty sure it was after four, maybe even after five in the morning.

Sitting there, she relished the dark, shadowy calm, what lights there were from town soothing her from a distance. As she'd mock-testified, she had no idea what Frank had been doing during those all-night shifts. When she'd asked him, he said it was a new job at the plant that would likely turn into an even better job down-the-line.

Ginger couldn't remember if Frank had told her, or whether she just assumed that Lowell Felker was behind the project. But then Felker was behind everything at Mentex. For some reason, Frank liked him or at least thought Lowell could do something for him. Ginger had no respect whatsoever for the man. At a company picnic one year he told a joke; she couldn't recall the whole set-up, but the punch line had the word pussy in it. All the men had laughed, Frank included, but Ginger wasn't amused. She didn't like to judge people but she didn't like crudeness, especially in ego-tripping men.

Angie Prez obviously felt that Mentex had violated some laws, that they were vulnerable, maybe even desperate. The question was, how much might they be willing to pay? Forget Angie Prez and her class action suit. Ginger knew exactly what the woman's game was. Prez wasn't rich herself but was, nonetheless, an intellectual snob who saw people like Ginger as beneath her, tools she could use to further her cause. During Frank's life, someone like Prez wouldn't have even talked to him and now she was out to avenge his death.

Prez's questions made Ginger uncomfortable. The woman wouldn't let go until she had turned over every rock, peeked into every dark corner and Ginger knew she couldn't go along with that. If there was money to be made from Mentex, why should Ginger have to share it with a bunch of strangers from all over the globe, not to mention Ms. Prez herself? That's why she called the plant as soon as she left Prez's office and invited Lowell Felker to come see her.

* * *

Lowell and Vance were standing beside the black Escalade, barbequed ribs and assorted sides on paper plates and in plastic containers spread out on the hood. Surrounding them was a rugged, arid space. "Not very pretty," uttered Vance.

Lowell chuckled as he shoved a plastic forkful of coleslaw into his open mouth. "Doesn't have to be pretty, man. Just has to be fertile down below." He swept his hand in front of him, indicating the space. "We can drill about sixty well pads here. It'll be as our test site until we get the process down perfect and then expand. Once this patch's served its purpose, all the permanent operations will be about a hundred yards over yonder."

Vance laughed. "Only you could look at this and spin it into gold, boss."

Lowell beamed. "See, the thing that isn't perfected is the cement casings that hold in the natural gas. They tend to crack while you're drilling. Hell, boy, we're in the cement business already, only from here on in, it's all for ourselves. Once we've got it down to a science we can use Dwight Shevney's family connections and supply fracking cement to every oil and gas company all over the world. It's like they're making the Coca-Cola but we're supplying the freaking bottles… Donaldson, that engineer I brought in, thinks that well we set up at the plant is only going to be good for a few more tests. That's why we need to annex this land to the town and get clear of Mentex."

"We've got to get the new mayor on board."

"I can handle Wiggins."

"What about Wendt?"

"What about him?"

"That guy's been trouble since the day he got here. If he helps Mexico City find out what we've been doing…" His voice trailed off, as if in search of how to finish the thought.

"Sonofabitch ain't married, is he?"

"What's that got to do with anything?"

Lowell chuckled. "You don't think he's queer, do you?"

"I heard he was married at one time," he said. "Wife croaked or something."

"I'll put some thought into how we can pull the rug out from under him."

Vance set down the rib he'd been working on. "Long as we're talking about potential shit-storms, you sure this meeting with Kincaid's wife is the right thing?"

Lowell wiped his hands with a paper cloth. "That meddlesome bitch Angie Prez has been trying to get her hooks into the woman, so the grieving widow probably wants to ask us a bunch of questions that Prez has put in her head. I've met Ginger Kincaid. She's a little church mouse and now that her old man's gone, she's poor as a church mouse. All that needs to happen today is to put a little cheese on the trap and believe me, she'll jump on it."

* * *

"Some more coffee?" asked Ginger. She was in an armchair in her living room, Lowell and Vance Dickason book-ending the couch.

"No thanks, Mrs. Kincaid," said Lowell. "Damned good coffee, though."

"It's just Nescafe," she said. Ginger was wearing a yellow, cotton dress with a green floral pattern. Nice, but not fancy. "I'm glad you came, Mr. Felker. I know how busy you are."

Lowell set his coffee cup atop the chipped, mismatching saucer. "And I'm glad you reached out to us, as I've been meaning to get in touch. Ever since coming to Mentex, coming to Lynton, I've considered the men and women who work for me as family. And with Frank gone, Mentex wants to make sure that you and your daughters have as many options and resources as possible."

Ginger looked at Lowell and when he realized she wasn't going to immediately respond, he pushed forward.

"What I'm saying is, Ginger, what I came here to say... if you're in need of something to ease the pain of Frank's passing, I'm sure we could find you a position at Mentex. Something substantial, lucrative even, but not demanding." He beamed. "Like I said, we like to take care of family."

Still nothing from her. Lowell couldn't help it; he glanced over at Vance who was staring at Ginger Kincaid.

She offered a thin smile. "That's very thoughtful, Mr. Felker. Generous, even. Trouble is, it's not really a job I'm looking for."

"*Looking for?*" Lowell echoed.

Ginger had rehearsed this moment. She'd never been good at confrontation, but with everything on the line, knew she couldn't falter. "Frank told me, before he died, what you were up to at the plant."

Lowell shifted on his haunches. He smiled tightly and shook his head. "I don't know what you're talking about."

"Those overnight shifts. You think that as close as Frank and I were, I'd let him be away all night without having him tell me exactly what he – what *you* – were doing?"

Lowell's look had clouded into a glare. "What we're doing at the plant is what we've always been doing – making cement. If this is some kind of a shakedown, Mrs. Kincaid, it isn't going to fly. Your husband worked at Mentex, but died here at home. End of story. I came here today out of respect for Frank and out of concern for you and your kids."

"No, you came to offer some kind of bribe I'm not going to take. Not with all I know." Ginger stood. "You're going to have to come up with more than some b.s. job to keep me quiet. So go off and think about it. Then come back with something I might find more acceptable."

* * *

Ginger was in Kent Kincaid's bed. She usually loved being there, loved the passion and delight they'd always found in each other ever since their affair began over a year before; at first, long distance, and then after Kent moved to town. But tonight she was worried and distracted. They'd just finished and were catching their breath.

Kent fired up a Basic.

"I've got Welker right where I want him," said Ginger, "and that Prez woman is going to ruin everything."

"Well, she suspects something, that's for sure."

"We need that money from Mentex and can't have anyone knowing about you and me until more time's passed. What would the kids think? We'd never be able to have a life together."

She reached over and he automatically handed her the cigarette.

"She all but asked me if you were at my house when Frank died," said Kent. "If you're not of any use to her, she might go ahead and tell anybody anything."

Ginger took a deep drag which made her voice husky. "We need to stop her."

"Stop her, like how?"

"She acts tough, but I'll bet she'd cut and run the first sign of anybody getting in her face." Ginger passed the cigarette back to Kent. "So... could you?"

"Could I what?"

"Get her to back off. Let her know if she starts wagging her tongue, it might turn out to be more trouble than it's worth."

"I guess I could put a scare into her."

"Not hurt her. But let her know if she starts spreading anything – getting hurt is a real possibility. You could do that, right, sugar?"

A Thousand Eyes

CHAPTER 19

Lonnie Elkins was making his way along the river, flashlight in hand, to meet up with the Bridge Buddies. The club had started a little more than three years before, near the end of seventh grade. The original members had been Lonnie and SB. A couple of others, Noah and Earl, joined later that summer. At first it had been exclusively boys, but then the twins, Iona and Babs, joined in, and Meg was the most recent addition. Others would come and go, but this was the core group. One or two nights a week, the Buddies would meet at the river, under the bridge. There was a spot where the bank jutted out forming a small island and unless it had rained a lot and the water got too high, the island was where they'd meet and talk and drink beer or smoke pot.

They would often head out and scale the cyclone fence to skateboard in the tiny skatepark next to the library, or go to the Willoughby farm on the edge of town and play water-tag in their fifty-meter pool. They'd go on reconnaissance missions as well; tossing rocks on the roofs of houses or rifling glove compartments of cars that had been foolishly left unlocked.

For the most part, it was easy getting out for the night. The Buddies wouldn't meet until midnight, so those who hadn't told their respective adults they were sleeping over at so-and-so's would simply slip out a little before twelve, then slip back in a little after four.

Lonnie had never been anywhere besides northern Colorado, but that suited him fine. He'd turned sixteen in March and effectively quit school after that. He lived with his old man, who would sooner or later force Lonnie to get more than just spotty, short-term jobs and start pulling his weight for real, but for now, Lonnie was content to remain kingpin of the Bridge Buddies, lording over their nocturnal mischief.

Lonnie was a few hundred feet from the bridge when his

flashlight picked up something glowing in one of the trees across the river. He stopped. What the hell was it?

A pair of green eyes was looking down on him.

And what the hell was gleaming behind it? Another pair. He waved the flashlight as though it were some magic wand and he was stunned to see more iridescent green eyes gazing back from every branch on that tree and the trees on either side of it. What the hell did those eyes belong to?

And then he heard splashing in the water and trained the light down on the river. A group of raccoons, five, six of them, were coming out of the water on the opposite bank. Lonnie knew from his years on the river that raccoons didn't like to swim, didn't like how heavy it made their thick coats, but they could and would swim when they had to. And these were now scaling up the trunk of that massive tree to join those scores of others who were perched upon branches. They'd have all blended in except for those green glowing eyes being picked up by the light.

And they just kept staring at him. Lonnie decided to get out of there; the whole thing was too spooky.

On his way to the bridge, he decided not to mention it to SB or any other Buddies. They'd say he was exaggerating, saying, okay, maybe you saw a half-dozen of them, but not what you're claiming, fifty or sixty. They might want to troop back there and the last thing Lonnie wanted was to see all those eyes again. The whole thing freaked him out. He'd never seen anything like it and never wanted to again.

* * *

"What's it gonna be tonight, Lon?" asked Sizeable Bill. SB was six-five and weighed two-sixty. Besides him and Lonnie, the crew for that night included the twins, Iona and Babs, who looked similar, but were not identical. Both were pretty girls with fair skin, but Iona had light hair and her eighteen-minutes-younger sister was a brunette. They were different in temperament, too. Iona tended to be cautious and watchful, a natural observer. Babs wasn't known as 'Mental Babs' for nothing.

"I've been working at the Chink Palace all week," Lonnie told everyone, "reinforcing the roof. There's a big hole up there with a temporary covering. It'll be easy as hell to climb up, drop in, grab some fortune cookies or whatever goofy stuff old man Chen's got in there."

"Maybe we could go into the kitchen and cook up some sushi," said Mental Babs.

"You don't know what you're talking about, girl," said her sister. "Sushi's Japanese and you don't heat it up."

"They serve beer there don't they?" said SB. "Let's lift some golden boys out of the cooler."

* * *

As Wolfpaw was nearing the China Palace, he felt a twinge of disappointment that Chen had not included him when he put together his renovation crew. When he could afford it, Wolfpaw would eat there, sometimes twice a week. So part of him, when he became aware of the movement on the roof of the restaurant, thought, *good, somebody's busting in to rob the place.* But then he knew it was just those kids, the ones who'd been drinking and smoking weed under the bridge these past few years. They'd always kept a wary distance, but he didn't like them, even suspected them of poking their noses into his trailer when he'd been out one night. Still, he didn't want to get distracted, had bigger things to worry about. He trained his eyes ahead and kept walking, giving the sense he hadn't seen them. But he'd seen them, even knew there were five of them up there, crouched in the shadows, breathing a little faster than they had been.

* * *

"I tell you that guy saw us," Iona was saying. "We need to get out of here."

"So what if he did?" said Lonnie. "He's nothing but an old coot. We even raided his crummy trailer once. Who's he gonna tell, and who's gonna listen to him?"

"Hey," Sizeable Bill called over. "What about this tarp? Help me get it off here."

"Are we gonna have to jump down some dark hole?" asked Iona. "How far down is it?"

"Don't turn into a princess," said Mental Babs. "Go grab a corner."

"Hang on a minute," said Lonnie, a hint of alarm in his tone.

And then a woman's voice commanded, "Come down off that roof, one at a time!"

After spotting the ladder on the side of the restaurant, Cinda had cruised up the alley, headlights off, and now was out of her SUV, a powerful flashlight trained on the figures above.

"Oh, shit," said Iona.

And now there were more lights, an alarming swirl of red and blue, speeding toward them.

CHAPTER 20

Leaving her office after working well into the evening, Angie Prez saw a pair of headlights swing out behind her.

She'd had a stalker a few years before, Charles Rogan, a self-styled activist who'd imposed himself into her life with way too many e-mails and phone calls after he'd contacted the Colorado Angels web site. He'd turned up at her office one afternoon with flowers and Angie was so flabbergasted she simply stepped by him, claiming she was on her way to a meeting. She hadn't felt she was dealing with the Uni-bomber, but there was a look in his eyes that unsettled her. She talked to Melissa, a Boulder cop friend of hers, about whether she should get a restraining order. "I wouldn't go that route," Melissa told her. "It just establishes that he's really got your attention, that you have some kind of relationship."

"So what do I do?" Angie had asked.

"Get a permit and learn how to use what you're carrying."

Although she'd done just that, she never heard from Rogan again, yet this was why she kept a nine millimeter Glock in her glove box.

She turned onto Broadway, one of the main tributaries of Boulder. The lights stayed behind her all the way, until she turned right on Table Mesa. Her eyes on the mirror, she noted that the car, which looked like a compact, kept going. But it didn't give her any sense of relief. She needed to turn left onto Yale, the street her building was on, then pull into the open parking lot in back. If whoever was following her had staked out the scene, they could be waiting.

Angie had to decide whether to park in the lot, then head into the back entrance or drive around until she felt more at ease. She started getting angry. This was her place, her home; she wasn't going to be kept away. Not when she had a loaded weapon within reach.

She pulled into her spot, about twenty yards from the back entrance. Her handbag slung over her shoulder, Angie held her keys in her left hand, the Glock in her right. Three steps from the door, a figure stepped out from the bushes. "Angie Prez," said the male voice.

Angie raised her arm and leveled the Glock at the figure who stood about ten feet away. In the glow from the security light at the back of the building, she could see that he had on a red ski mask but held nothing in his hands.

"Whoa, wait. You've got this all wrong."

"You're the one who has it wrong, asshole. Take off that mask."

"Now wait a second, Miss. Perez. I'm only here to talk to you."

"Take the mask off…"

At that moment, Claire Smoltz, a young CU professor who lived down the hall from Angie, stepped outside, pulling a large suitcase behind her. She froze as she took in the scene. "What's going on? Should I call nine-one-one?"

Peeling off his ski mask, Kent Kincaid stood there gaping at Angie. "Will you put that gun away?" he uttered.

"Not on your life. Why the hell are you following me?"

"I just came to ask you to leave Ginger and me alone."

Angie took a step forward, pointing the gun at his forehead. "Ginger and *you*, huh?"

"Do you want me to make the call, Angie?" asked Claire.

"No, I can handle this."

Angie took another step toward Kent who involuntarily raised his hands in surrender. "I just came here to talk," he whined.

"Okay, start talking. Tell me about you and Ginger."

"Look," Kent sputtered. "I know what we've done isn't right, but we're really truly in love. We couldn't help it… And we were gonna tell Frank, but it just wasn't time yet. We never dreamed he was gonna, you know..."

Claire took a last look at the scene, then, once again pulling the suitcase, hurried toward her car.

Angie stepped even closer to Kent. Part of her felt like laughing, and part of her felt like pulling the trigger. "You're pathetic, you know that? Get out of here, asshole. You make me sick. Ginger too. Just get out so I can go upstairs and take a shower. Talking to you makes my skin crawl."

CHAPTER 21

Set back off Highway 64, between Lynton and Valmont, an orange neon sign that said *Rudy's* glowed over a sprawling gravel parking lot.

When Todd drove up a few minutes before ten p.m. there were several vehicles parked haphazardly, a few of them pick-ups and SUVs with oversized wheels that looked as though a gun-rack would come as standard equipment. As Todd approached the front door, he could hear a throbbing rhythm from inside. He entered a tight and narrow entranceway to have his hand scraped with some ultra-violet substance. A young woman in a top hat and heavy eyeliner and little else led him to a table near the front of the stage. "Not here," Todd told her. "Off to the side, please."

She led him to an even dimmer part of the dim room.

Onstage, two young women, one a strapping blonde and one a tiny Asian, were gyrating in slomo to some tune from the heyday of music videos. *"Ain't no doubt about it, you're addicted to love...."*

"What'll it be, hon?"

A woman, who, even in the altered light, looked at least twenty years older than the onstage tag team, was standing beside his table.

"I'll have a beer... in a bottle please."

Face impassive, pencil at the ready, she uttered, "Coors, Coors Light, Bud, Bud Light, MGD or Miller Lite..." A bored conductor rattling off stops.

Todd considered this for a second, then said, "I don't care, surprise me."

"Well that's a first." She strode away on stiletto heels.

Todd glanced around the poorly lit space. He had no notion of who he might be there to meet. No one else had come in.

He'd been to a few strip clubs during his film days in L.A. but always felt they were desperate and ridiculous, especially the audience. Once, he'd had to attend a young actor's birthday party at some joint on Santa Monica Boulevard and it ended up on TMZ, complete with a shot of Todd at a table grinning in the background as the birthday boy cavorted with a trio of dancers. Rene had not been pleased.

His beer arrived, a Miller Lite as it turned out. The music had changed to some kind of trance instrumental and the two dancers were doing to each other what each had been doing to their respective poles. Todd was genuinely distracted by it, for when his attention turned back to the table to take a fresh sip of beer, the chair across from him was occupied. Again, Todd wasn't sure who he'd been expecting but this was a slight, dark-haired woman in her early twenties, wearing what looked to be a tan trench coat. "Hello there," said Todd.

The woman was pretty and smiled a pretty smile. "Buy me a drink?"

"Sure," Todd responded.

The waitress came back to the table. "Something else here?"

"A white Russian," said the young woman.

"You got it."

And then there was nothing for a while except the trance beat and this stranger across from him. Finally, Todd said, "Maybe you can tell me what happens next."

"Next?" said the woman.

"I'm not much for this cloak and dagger stuff."

The white Russian arrived and the woman took a sip. "Ever had one of these?"

"No," said Todd.

"I don't really like to drink but this is like candy. You can barely taste the booze."

"Like I said, what happens next?"

The young woman was smiling again. "I'm a scout, kind

of, who needed to make sure you showed. Now I'll go get the person you really need to talk to and they'll come and sit down." She drew the glass to her lips and upended it, draining all but the ice cubes. "Don't go anywhere. They'll be here in a minute, and you're gonna want to hear what they have to say."

She rose from the table and Todd watched her tightening the belt to her trench coat as she moved toward the exit.

* * *

A half-hour later, Todd was nursing a second beer he hadn't really wanted when he determined that no one was coming to meet him. He left a generous tip and headed out the way he'd come in.

He walked to his car, attuning his senses to whether anyone was following him but there was no evidence of that. The whole excursion had been a bust; driving out to the middle of nowhere to meet no one and come up with nothing.

The drive back was dark with an empty feeling to everything. He considered going to Ossie's for a nightcap but didn't feel like talking to anyone. He felt tired and maybe, he thought, he'd actually go right to sleep for a change.

Todd pulled into the open carport. Getting out of the car, he freshly realized that, since his animal encounters, he'd gotten into the habit of looking around when he arrived home. He'd thought of telling Cinda Rigg about the possum visit. Maybe it supported her Mentex theory, maybe he'd just left the window open. Yet he recalled that as the possum's weight was *pressing against his chest*, its black eyes were staring into his and something passed through his mind as it was happening. Those eyes had not been hostile. Something about them was probing, as though posing a question beyond language or understanding. Even thinking about it was just too weird, so he hadn't told Cinda Rigg nor anyone else. Maybe a shrink... in about twenty years.

This night, nothing was stirring, nothing he could detect at least. The open space of Juniper Park, the looming mountains beyond, the babbling river, were all becoming soothingly familiar.

He climbed the small set of steps to the wooden porch. Key in hand, he fitted it into the lock. The entrance was dark, he flipped the switch and the living room was cast in light. Todd was relieved to be home. He would have preferred that his little outing had borne some kind of fruit, but it had proven to be yet another confounding piece to an already confounding summer.

He stepped into the kitchen and turned on the light, wanting a glass of water before turning in. He grabbed a tall glass from the cabinet and placed it under the filter. As the water flowed into the glass, Todd noted two other glasses on the counter. They were his, or rather they had come with the cottage, but the half-filled fifth of vodka had not. There was also a tiny bottle, a vial that was unmarked.

He looked over and froze. Filling the open entrance to the kitchen was the young dark-haired woman from the bar. Only now she wasn't wearing her trench coat, but was clad in jeans and a faded, blue t-shirt. "What the hell are you doing here?" Todd managed.

The young woman didn't respond. Todd's mind spun. Was she alone? He stepped toward her. "How the hell did you get in?"

She still didn't say anything but took a step toward Todd, something in her hand. Next he felt that his face, his eyes, were on fire. His hands went up as his mouth and his nose felt aflame and he sank to his knees. "What the hell did you do?" he uttered, or tried to, as the words tangled into a violent cough.

Todd struggled to catch his breath. Everything around him was blurred and he wondered if he'd ever regain his sight. Dimly, from the living room, he could hear the woman. "As quick as you can," she was saying in a voice that sounded anything but urgent. "Yes, I will, but hurry."

* * *

Lying in bed, trying to sleep, Angie Prez had a blindfold over her eyes, a practice she'd picked up during a summer of perpetual daylight, years before, in Alaska. She was drifting into sleep when her cell rang. She slipped the blindfold off before answering. The voice on the other end said: "Angie Prez?"

"Yes?"

"It's Todd Wendt. We met the other night at Ossie's."

"Yes?"

"I work for Mentex."

"I know. Why are you calling at this hour? Why are you *calling*?"

"I need a lawyer, and I hope you're a damned good one."

CHAPTER 22

Todd was able to post bail to the charge of aggravated battery. Upon his release from custody, Todd slept through the day and Angie came to his place in the late afternoon. They sat down and Angie opened her laptop.

"Faye Sorrento, twenty, of Valmont, Colorado, says she met you earlier last night at Rudy's Bachelor Club."

"That's right. She seated herself at my table, although she never told me her name."

"She says you arranged a date with her. That is, she agreed to come back here with you. She left her car in Rudi's parking lot at your suggestion and you drove her here in your car."

"That's totally bullshit."

"I've run a check on Ms. Sorrento," said Angie, glancing down at her laptop. "Enrolled at Foothills Community College and employed by the Star-shine Housecleaning Service. Her only prior conviction is for stealing a pair of running shoes when she was seventeen. I was hoping for solicitation or some related charge but unfortunately, there's nothing like that."

Todd didn't say anything. Just sipped the decaf he'd made for them.

"The waitress at Rudy's Bachelor's Club, Crystal Crawford is her current name, saw you talking with Ms. Sorrento, who claims she felt uncomfortable with the scene at Rudy's but agreed to go back to your place for a nightcap with the understanding that you'd drive her back to get her car before one a.m. She walked into the kitchen while you were pouring the drinks and confronted you about the vial that was on the counter. When she tried to leave, you grabbed her arm and a struggle ensued. She was able to free herself and use the pepper spray she keeps in her bag."

"Bullshit. All of it."

"The substance on your counter, suspected to be GHB, commonly known as the date rape drug, has been sent for testing to the county lab."

"This is insane. I was totally set up."

"If that's the case, you should have gotten one whiff of Rudy's and run the hell out of there."

Todd didn't respond, having thought exactly that more than a few times.

"And there's something else."

Todd looked at her and waited.

"Your personal computer at Mentex has been checked out by the county authorities and there's direct evidence of you going to Faye Sorrento's Facebook Page and arranging a meeting with her. What that adds up to," Angie added, "is prior access and motivation."

"Somebody went into my office and did that."

"Mentex is behind this, is that what you're saying? How did she get in here?"

"Mentex owns this place. Somebody gave her a key."

Angie shut down her laptop. "I need to know everything, Todd. Something you think may not be important may turn out to be *very* important."

Todd's cell phone chimed. He looked down at the caller ID, then said to Angie. "Speak of the devil. I should take this."

"Okay, but, not a word about the case."

"Hello," Todd said.

The voice on the other end sounded breezy and animated. "Wendt, Lowell Felker here. I just got a call from Symington over at the Weekly Record." He laughed harshly. "What the hell kind of a mess have you got yourself into?"

* * *

The following morning, Todd opened his laptop and found a

message in his mailbox marked *Urgent! Subject: Alleged Incident.*
Sender: *Human Resources, Mentex International.*

To Todd Wendt:

Having been informed of the recent and unfortunate allegations involving yourself and a female resident of Colorado (USA), Mentex International has decided that you are to report to our Houston facility, effective immediately. This action is of course subject to the terms of your impending charges and in no way reflects upon your guilt or innocence. We have simply determined that for all concerned: you, Mentex International , and Mentex-Colorado, it would be prudent that you resume your duties from a more neutral locale, being granted leave to participate in any legal proceedings related to this matter.

Please note that Mr. Sandoval, who is still currently at sea, was reached regarding what has been determined to be an urgent situation and has approved the course of action noted above.

Sincere Regards,

Elena Odeo, Director, Human Resources

Herman Sandoval, Chief Executive Officer, cc'd.

Todd shut down his laptop and got out of his bathrobe. He showered and, while the physical effects of the pepper spray had all but receded, he still felt stunned. He needed to feel that he was thinking straight, making sound decisions.

After fixing himself toast and coffee and a bowl of cornflakes, he ate and drank slowly, making a conscious choice to not turn on the radio or television, wanting his mind to be as clear as possible.

Sometime after noon he set out, walking through town, turning left off Peach Valley Road to Burnham Park, then another left to walk up and down each of the main streets on the north side of town, crossing North Center Street, then Eagle Lane, then doubling back until he was on Porter Boulevard, which resembled no boulevard he'd ever seen, but was a sleepy, leafy street ending in a cul-de-sac where the river veered beside it. Todd's eye was caught by a wooden sign in the tidy lawn of the house at the end of that street: *Apartment for rent*.

He went up to the front door of a white, one-story house. A woman of around seventy answered, dressed in an apricot-shaded, summery dress as though she expected company. "Yes?" she said with a smile.

"You have a place for rent?"

She smiled. "It's in the back. Just one floor, I'm afraid. Over the garage, although I don't use the garage."

"May I have a look?"

"Well, surely. Let me get the key."

Todd waited while the woman bustled around inside. When she returned, she led him through an impeccably tended back yard. "I haven't rented it for over five years, but you know how things are. I'm on a fixed income and I can use some extra money. I'm Sylvia Walthrop, by the way."

Todd introduced himself and she led him through a small, tight breezeway and, without entering the garage proper, up a flight of wooden steps.

The space was entirely open, sparsely but effectively furnished, bookshelves on two of the four walls and the furthest wall overlooking the river. Todd knew immediately he would like that proximity, having grown accustomed to the soothing sound of the rushing current at night. There was a musty odor which he felt would disappear once some fresh air was let in.

"I need to confess, Mr. Wendt, that when Garrett and I, he was my late husband, converted this space fifteen years ago, I'm not sure it was entirely legal. The town doesn't know it's back here, and we'd need to keep whatever arrangement we come to quiet – that is, if you decide to move in. I didn't list it or anything, just put that sign in the yard. It's, oh, I don't know, six hundred a month plus whatever utilities you end up using. There's electric baseboard heating if you end up staying into the winter. We could try a month-to-month arrangement to see if it works out."

Todd looked at her, offering a smile of his own. "Can I move in today?"

Mrs. Walthrop agreed and Todd walked back to the Mentex cottage and packed his two suitcases, left his keys under the mat in the Malibu and trudged the few blocks to his new residence.

He unpacked and, as the afternoon drew down, lay on the bed and listened to the river, feeling the breeze come through the open screens. He fired up his laptop and sent a reply to Mentex International, telling them that he would not be coming back to headquarters that he was, in fact, resigning.

Todd lay back on the bed. There was an overhead fan and he watched it for a while, imagining it was a helicopter, hovering above him. He was in the field, on a solo mission and the enemy was out there, commanded by Lowell Felker. They had provisions, resources, weapons; he was all but alone, a stranger in a strange land. How could he have been so stupid to walk into a trap like that? He needed to fight back.

When he awoke it was dark. For several distressing seconds he had no idea where he was until some coherent sequence of events washed over him. He was in a new place, he remembered, and he was in trouble. Getting slowly off the bed, he made his way to the love seat that he turned so it faced the alley, the brush and the river. He could hear water rushing over rocks. It hadn't rained for days but the river sounded vigorous. Mrs. Walthrop had mentioned a motion light behind the garage and now Todd, in his half-asleep state, realized that was what had rustled him off the bed. The light was glowing but there was no evidence that anything was lurking in the alley or probing the garbage cans. Todd sat there looking until the light blinked out on its own.

He went back to bed, this time beneath the covers. Damn, he was tired but sleep seemed elusive. There was no light on in the big open room. Then this feeling came over him that somehow, he was being watched.

Feeling vaguely silly, in a kind of crouch, he crept to the window. There was a screen over it and he felt a subtle breeze.

Nothing out there but leaves and branches, sky and moonlight. The stars were hiding tonight. It was overcast and Todd hoped it would rain to cool things off. He was looking at the scene, not focused on anything in particular, just holding a soft gaze as he took in the shadows and light.

He recalled a photograph that Rene had taken one night when they'd been driving through Los Angeles. There was an old man sitting at a bus stop and Rene insisted they pull over so she could snap his picture.

When she developed the print, a phantom image appeared. A previous shot, taken when they'd been in Italy, showed a man in broad daylight, looking out over an open field. Somehow that image, the last Rene had captured on their trip, imprinted itself on the next shot in that same roll of film. The result was eerie.

This is what Todd was thinking because he felt he saw a phantom image before his eyes. Some guy – tall, scrawny, a floppy hat – half-concealed beside the trunk of a tree on the bank of the river.

But no, he was tired, was seeing things.

CHAPTER 23

Todd knew his best hope was to prove Mentex had motivation to set him up, that they were indeed up to something they only wanted a select number of people to know about. He was beginning to suspect that whatever it was might well have been beyond the practices of Mentex International itself, something that Lowell Felker was in charge of and clearly benefiting from. He was thinking this on his way to his first formal strategy meeting with Angie. Upon moving, he'd given up the car Mentex provided and hadn't decided whether he would replace it. Having arranged to meet Angie at her office, he'd taken the bus to Boulder.

Once they settled in for the meeting, Todd spilled it, the friction between him and Lowell Felker, how he'd discovered that Mentex was engaged in some kind of surreptitious project that didn't appear on the books, including what he'd witnessed when the elk caused the truck to tip over that Sunday night.

Angie sat up a little higher. "And you're sure they were hauling water out there?"

"It spilled all over the place. If it'd been toxic that driver and I would have been as dead as Frank Kincaid. But whatever they were going to mix it with was right there at the plant."

Todd expected Angie to lay out a course of action that included finding out who all the extra hands were that Felker had on site after hours; where the trucks were coming from, and why the project was kept off the books and under the cover of night. But Angie said nothing like that. Instead she asked, "Do you want a cold drink?"

"Sure," Todd said.

Angie went over to a small refrigerator and came up with two bottles of designer root beer. "This is my secret vice. Can't get enough of the stuff."

She filled two glasses with ice and poured.

When she handed one to Todd, he took a sip. "So what do you think about what I just told you?"

Angie took a sip of her own, then said, "I think I can't be your lawyer anymore."

This was the last thing Todd was expecting. "You think I'm lying?"

"You're facing sexual assault charges. What you're saying about Mentex and some secret project will be deemed irrelevant and inadmissible."

"But whatever they're involved in, I poked around it, so they set me up."

Angie shook her head. "We try to go after Mentex the way you're suggesting and we'll be laughed out of court." She went over to her desk. "I'm going to put you in touch with Mia Dolenz, the finest criminal defense attorney in this region."

"I don't want a new attorney. I want you."

Angie shook her head. "Sorry, Todd. My specialty is labor. You don't wanna be taking a knife to a gunfight."

* * *

Dale Wiggins was at Spokes, his bike shop, when Lowell Felker ambled in. Dale had a mountain bike up on the rack, repairing an inner-tube, and didn't convey much need to interrupt the task. "What can I help you with?" he said, by way of a greeting.

"I've been meaning to tell you," said Lowell, spinning the front wheel on an elevated cruiser that was on sale. "That Criterium race you tried to get off the ground two summers ago was a hell of an idea."

Dale looked at him warily but was, he couldn't help himself, interested.

Lowell continued, "We're living in an outdoors paradise, right at the foot of the Rockies. I think your instincts were correct; cyclists would come from all over to participate. Call it the Spokes Annual Crit, or something like that."

Finished with the tire, Dale sat down at his workbench. "I lost money on that, I don't have the funds for that kind of investment."

Lowell laughed. "Hell, Mentex will put up the money. We'd arrange all the additional sponsors, publicize the whole thing state-wide as well as nationally, even internationally. We need tax write-offs and this is exactly the kind of high-profile project we can get behind. If we commit to this now, we'd be ready to go a year from Labor Day. It'd be perfect, start the summer with Lynton Frontier Days, then the music fest July fourth, and the bike race Labor Day weekend. We'd just need a face, and you're the natural spokesman, excuse the pun."

"I can't guarantee I'll still be in office then."

Lowell appeared just short of slapping Dale on the shoulder. "This has nothing to do with whether you're in office or not. We'll see to it the thing gets established as an annual event. After that, Mentex can transition to being just one of the sponsors and it can be your baby."

Like a man who'd just been shaken awake, Dale looked up at Lowell. "If you think something like this will keep me from looking into Mentex's environmental practices, you've got the wrong guy."

Lowell laughed. "When you gonna come by and tour the plant?"

"I'm pretty slammed," said Dale.

"Well, our doors are open. Wide open for you, Mr. Mayor. If you don't call next week, I'm gonna keep coming by till you take me up on my offer."

Dale watched him go. The guy was a snake, totally full of shit. But ever since Dale opened his mouth that night at the town hall, his misgivings about taking office had been growing. Interested in politics, but no politician. *Cycling, though...* He grabbed the pump to inflate the tire he'd just patched. *The Spokes Annual Crit...* That was something he could get behind.

CHAPTER 24

The Bridge Buddies had a shack they'd built, hidden in the brush along the river. In it were stashed all kinds of things: a few cases of beer lifted from outside the Blues n' Brew, kitchen matches and lighter fluid palmed from the Center Street Grocery; a couple of cans of paint and a few brushes from the hardware store; rain slickers Lonnie had stolen from the nearly blind old guy who ran the fly fishing shop.

Lonnie emerged from the makeshift hut and tugged on a pair of muddy fishing boots. Nobody else had shown up yet. He had to admit that the bust had slowed things down. The semi-regulars seemed to have faded. Only SB had come around regularly. But Lonnie did expect to see the twins tonight, as their parents had gone to Utah for the weekend and their aunt, who was pretty clueless, could be slipped out on easily.

The night they were busted, only Lonnie Elkins and SB were charged. The twins had been released to the custody of their parents, they were only fifteen and had no previous record. This was SB's second arrest and Lonnie's third, misdemeanors in each case: petty theft, disturbing the peace. The Boulder County DA was all set to file for criminal trespassing and malicious mischief. Lonnie was poised to plead not guilty, would claim he'd left some tools at the work site and the others were just helping him retrieve them. Old man Chen decided not to press charges, claiming that Elkins and Covington were "good boys underneath" who'd promised reparations that included re-paving his parking lot and painting the restaurant's exterior throughout the rest of the summer.

Chen's fear of them had saved Lonnie and SB from a stretch in the Youth Correctional Facility.

Lonnie waded into the river at the spot where the tubers would slide over a smooth and over-sized flat rock. He enjoyed feeling the water swirl around his legs, all the way up beyond his ankles, to the middle of his thighs. It was kind of a rush and he did some of his best thinking just standing like that. He hadn't done much fishing since he'd been around fourteen or so, but it reminded him of those times his old man would take him into the mountains and they'd cast side-by-side in a creek or a river, not talking much, each in his own private world. There was that one time though, Lonnie had been eight or nine, when the old man told him about the Snap Monster.

He'd first heard of it, the old man said, when he'd been around Lonnie's age. The old man grew up in Lynton and claimed to know every secret of its red earth and rushing water. The Snap Monster was part mammal and part amphibian, a remnant of the age before the appearance of humans. A descendant of water creatures who likely migrated from the Pacific Ocean, then were carried through the American West by the Colorado River, its massive shell covered as much ground as a tent. They'd tried to survive on land, but most of them didn't make it. The few that did crawled into the rivers and there they stayed, feeding on trout, much to the displeasure of the region's fishermen. Now there was only one Snap Monster left. Rarely seen, it was able to hold its breath under the current for hours or even days at a time. It could plant itself below the surface, its entire shell submerged in mud. When it needed to breathe, the Snap Monster would extend its neck up several feet, like some sort of rubbery crane, for just enough time to fill its massive lungs with mountain air. Fortified, it would dip below again, to continue its assault on the trout population. The Snap Monster would eat anything, but trout was what it hunted.

Had Lonnie's old man ever seen it? Just once, when he was a kid himself, for the blink of an eye. The rushing water had eddied and a head as big around as a truck inner tube had appeared, sucking air ferociously, rearing up to reveal a massive shell, covered in algae and shaded green like a camouflage jacket, before plunging back below the surface.

Around thirteen, Lonnie came to the conclusion that the Snap Monster was just his old man spinning another thing he knew nothing about. But sometimes when Lonnie was out here, especially when he was alone, he'd find himself scanning the surface for a glimpse of it.

Lonnie had a beer can in his left hand, one of those tall ones that Ossie Anderson cooked up right there in his pub. This wasn't Lonnie's first one of the night. He didn't like the taste all that much, preferring PBR or Bud Light, but the higher alcohol content in Ossie's more than did the trick. Having been drinking since around ten o'clock, it was now after midnight and Lonnie was pretty buzzed and had to take a leak. This was another thing he enjoyed about standing out there in the current, whipping it out and letting loose right into the river made him feel truly part of the flow.

He unzipped his jeans and was about five seconds into it when he sensed something to his right, a light being trained on him from the riverbank. At first he thought it was the cops, then realized it was the twins, announcing their arrival with that military spot Mental Babs would sometimes bring from their parents' garage. "You crazy bitch, turn that light off!" But he wasn't angry, was glad that somebody else had turned up.

High on the bank, crouched in the brush, Iona and Mental Babs were giggling.

"My God," said Iona, "it looks like *he's* the one holding the flashlight."

"What did I tell you?"

"It gets even bigger? Who would let him shove that into them?"

"That woman who runs the nail salon supposedly can't get enough of Lonnie. She must be, what, twenty years older than him? And I heard that Lauren Batholemew tried but ended up just getting him off by using both hands."

"Have you ever seen SB's before? I'll bet he's got one even bigger."

"We all went skinny dipping once. He's got muscles and all, but not where Lonnie has his."

"What are you two laughing about? Turn off that light and get down here."

"Put that thing away, Lonnie," Mental Babs called out. "It's an unconcealed weapon."

Lonnie laughed as he shook it off a few times, then tucked it in and zipped up. He wasn't interested in either of the twins, at least not in that way. He preferred grown women who'd seen their share and truly appreciated his God-given gift. His first had been his babysitter, over twice his age, when he'd been eleven. Long after his old man stopped hiring her, she'd come by at times she felt sure only Lonnie would be at home. By the time he was fourteen, Lonnie was tired of her. When he told her to leave him alone, she'd actually broken down and cried.

The twins came down the bank just as Lonnie was stepping out of the water.

"Anybody else coming tonight?" he asked.

"It's getting hard for Meg to sneak out," said Mental Babs.

"All right then," said Lonnie. "I say we go over to SB's place and toss some pebbles against his window."

They woke SB, then went out roaming, seeing what they could bump into. Lonnie was oddly quiet that night on the way back to the shack. It was only the next morning when he told SB what he'd lifted from the glove compartment of a pick-up truck.

"Yeah, but what do you want to do with it?"

Lonnie just smiled and said, "*In*-surance, man. Didn't you ever hear that saying – Better to have a gun and not need one, than need a gun and not have one."

* * *

Dale was at the Mentex plant, walking to where he'd parked his bicycle. Lowell Felker strode alongside of him.

"I hope you're leaving with the impression that I've been running a tight ship, Dale."

"It certainly appears that way, given that you're mixing cement here."

"How else we gonna build roads and office buildings, not to mention schools and hospitals, without getting our hands a little chalky?"

Dale stopped beside his bike. "It seems like you're doing what you can to contain any... what would you call it? Collateral damage."

Lowell gave a harsh laugh. "With this most recent wave of accusations, Mentex even sent our top public relations guy, Todd Wendt, I'm sure you've heard about him, to be on site for a spell. First day he got here, I gave him the same nook and cranny tour, and the man realized he was gonna have a lot of time on his hands. Too bad for him all that down time got him in trouble." Lowell took a moment, then asked, "Are you aware of whose jurisdiction the plant is under?"

"It's part of the county, I looked into it."

"Right, and that's why the people of Lynton can bitch and moan about us, but they can't really do dick." Lowell smiled. "We've made some missteps in the past, but frankly we're sick of all the ill-will and accusations." Lowell winked, then said, "I hope you've been thinking about that bike race, Dale."

CHAPTER 25

The Cowpoke Saloon was south of Valmont. Lowell had advised Iris not to play a shithole like that but, as usual, she wouldn't listen. Now, here she was, up there with just her mandolin, accompanied by Harlan Sievers, a skinny and perpetually stoned guitar player, who'd gig for the bar tab. She'd wanted Barry Quinn but the Cowpoke's owner wouldn't allow teenagers to gig there, no matter how good they were. The twenty or so patrons were largely ignoring her, engaged in conversation. Lowell had come alone and was at a table near the front, trying to look supportive as his lover was enduring indifference and disrespect. Three frat jocks at the table to his left, probably slumming from CU, were loudly commenting on Iris's performance.

"Look how she nearly eats up that microphone," one of them was saying. "If she opened her mouth all the way, I wonder if she could get the whole thing down her throat."

"I wonder if she could get it someplace else," another of them chortled.

"Oh, I bet she could, with room to spare."

"You could probably park a car in there."

"An SUV..."

"SUV, Stuffed-up vagina," one all but yelled, as the trio nearly collapsed on the floor with laughter.

Lowell had been reading the table for half-an-hour and knew that confronting them would surely escalate, but he needed to do something, or what kind of a pussy was he? Vance wasn't with him, but then Vance would be of no use in this kind of situation. The kid was loyal, probably loyal enough to get his ass kicked, but that wouldn't help anything. Lowell looked around the room. No bouncer in sight, just a pair of bored and weary waitresses. A few couples here and there, yakking, caught up in each other.

And then he spotted them.

A pair of guys, hanging in the open area that led into the room. He'd seen them any number of times in Lynton. Lowell didn't know their names but knew their reputations. They were tough and troubled and one of them looked six-six and must have tipped in at two-fifty. The other kid was short and stocky and had the eyes of a killer.

Lowell pushed back from his table and walked over to them. "Could I talk to you fellas a minute?"

Lonnie and SB didn't respond, just eyed him suspiciously. He pressed by them and into the tight, dingy hallway that led to the men's room.

"How would you boys like to make some money?"

The big one looked at the smaller guy, who kept his eyes on Lowell.

"See, fellas," Lowell continued, "that's a lady friend of mine up there, a very nice lady, and those assholes near the front are giving her a hard time. But if I take them on, it's three to one. I'm betting that if I enlisted you boys for say, fifty bucks apiece, we could invite them outside to the parking lot and wipe up the ground with them."

Before either of them could say anything, one of the frat jocks had pushed back from the table and was ambling in their direction. He had a smirk on his face but was oblivious to any plan being hatched. He said, "Scuse me," as he stepped by Lowell and Lonnie and SB, then ducked into the men's room.

"Tell you what, Mr. Felker," Lonnie droned. "Just wait right here and my buddy and me will take care of this without you getting your hands dirty."

Lowell was smiling. "You know me, huh?"

Lonnie smiled back. "Everybody knows you, Mr. Felker. Now don't move."

He and SB turned and stepped into the men's room. There was a half-minute of muffled sounds, including some banging and groaning, then Lonnie came out by himself, stepped by Lowell and went straight to where the two remaining frat jocks were sitting at their table.

"Don't mean to interrupt," said Lonnie, concern etched across his face. "But aren't you with that guy who just went into the head? Do you know if he's epileptic or something? He's having some kind of seizure."

They bolted out of their chairs. As soon as the men's room door opened, SB cracked the first one full in the face, blood spurting as the frat jock collapsed, then curled up desperately in response to SB's boots thudding into his ribs. Lonnie was right behind the other guy and kicked him behind his left kneecap, sending him down on one knee.

Lonnie booted him viciously in the middle of his back and, as the guy rolled over in stunned agony, Lonnie began jumping on his chest the way a kid would gleefully jump on a bed.

Lowell was in the room, having closed the door behind, and looked on in amazement as the Lynton boys did their work.

"Faggot!" yelled Lonnie to his nearly unconscious victim.

"Bitch!" shouted SB, as he inflicted even more damage to his already helpless opponent.

Guy Number One had rolled onto his back, face distorted, still trying to determine what was happening, and why. Lowell leaned down, deciding to clear that up for him. "*You're* the one with the big mouth, asshole."

He glanced into the corner and saw that a plunger had been unceremoniously stashed there. Lowell stepped over and grabbed it, taking it into one of the stalls where he shoved it into an un-flushed toilet. When he pulled it out, the plunger was dripping with fetid, brown and amber grime. He rushed back, then pressed it onto the first guy's face, covering his nose and mouth, holding it there for a good twenty seconds. Laughing in response to the muffled sounds the guy was making. He followed Lonnie and SB out to the parking lot where he handed

Lonnie a Franklin.

Lonnie, laughing his ass off, said, "We'll take the dough, Mr. Felker, but we'd a-done it for free."

* * *

The Lynton Town Hall was crowded for its monthly community meeting. Todd was seated in the back while Dale Wiggins was talking, the microphone on a small stand in front of him. "About North Center Street... For one thing, it's too narrow. Widening it even a couple of feet on both sides will help the flow of traffic. Plus, I'm in touch with a number of local artists who've volunteered to contribute some sculptures that we can install between the streets and the sidewalks. This will make it a lot more attractive."

An older man rose to his feet. "What about Third Street, the potholes? You seem to only be concerned about the traffic in front of your bike shop."

Dale recoiled as though he'd been pricked with a pin. "C'mon, Gil, that's not fair."

"The hell it isn't..."

"Mine isn't the only shop on North Center."

The mayor appeared to be off-center. Todd saw this as his moment and called out, "You got elected with a pledge to investigate Mentex. Whatever happened to that?"

Dale looked at him as though deeply offended. "I took a tour of the plant. There's nothing going on there that hasn't gone on there for years."

"I'll bet Lowell Felker conducted that tour. And I'm sure he showed you only what he wanted you to see."

Wiggins' face began to redden. "Didn't you get fired from Mentex, Mr. Wendt?"

"Actually I resigned."

Beverly Walsh called out, "The man has a point, Dale. Are

you really no longer concerned with what they might be cooking up at the plant?"

A guy wearing a Broncos cap pointed his finger at Dale. "How about coming over to my house and drinking a glass of tap water. Maybe you can go back to Mentex and find out what they're doing to make it taste like it's coated with Vaseline."

Dale's face was contorted as he picked up his gavel. "I move that we take a ten minute adjournment." He slammed the gavel and it echoed throughout the hall.

CHAPTER 26

Although she didn't let Todd in on it, after talking with him, Angie had strong suspicions about what was going on at the Mentex plant. For whatever reason, they were fracking, that's what the bastards were up to. Fracking had been deemed unlawful in two different county elections; she led the opposition against it both times. Angie didn't know how or why they'd gotten into it, but if she could substantiate her suspicions, it would be a grand slam. She'd nail a multi-national for practices they weren't sanctioned to be engaged in, she'd solve Frank Kincaid's death; it would be the culmination of everything she'd been fighting against since law school and before, a national and even international victory. It might even get Todd Wendt off the hook.

Angie had Billings, who worked in transportation, as her solid contact inside the Mentex operation and, since the covert activity was apparently taking place on the weekends, she got him to agree to meet her in the late afternoon on Friday, in his second floor office. Of course there would be no actual meeting. At the gate she told the guard, "Paula De Angeles, here to see Mr. Billings." It was unlikely she would be recognized but just to be safe, she'd pulled her hair back and donned her reading glasses.

Billings let her into his office, then allowed her access to a cleared-out storage closet when he left at the end of the day. With her laptop to keep her company, Angie hung in there for over three hours before slipping out.

The only sign of life in the dark hallway was that the cleaning crew had parked a cart of materials outside one of the offices. She didn't anticipate much trouble from any of the crew, Billings had assured her he'd encountered them many times after hours and they'd barely glanced at him. A massive glass window at the end of the hall overlooked the rear of the Mentex plant.

Looking down, Angie knew she'd struck pay dirt. There were lights and tanker trucks and a dozen workers down there. *Water. Water being brought in.* Angie was well-versed in the fracking process, had even been instrumental in banning it from Boulder County.

They'd mix the water with sand and chemicals, approximately forty thousand gallons for each action, to make their fracking fluid. Approximately six hundred chemicals went into the fluid: nasty stuff like uranium, mercury, radium, hydrochloric acid and formaldehyde. Then all of this was injected into the ground through a drilled pipeline. During the process, methane gas and toxic chemicals leak out and contaminate groundwater. Methane concentrations were as much as seventeen times higher in drinking water near fracking sites. Thirty to fifty percent of the fracking fluid was recovered, the rest was left in the ground. That's why people were complaining about the smell and taste of the water in Lynton. Something had to have gone wrong at the plant that night and Frank Kincaid was poisoned. You could be dead within an hour of direct exposure to fracking fluid.

There was some activity, a truck rumbling up. The truck was pulling an enclosed, unmarked tank and there were a half-dozen workers waiting for the massive vehicle to roll to a halt.

Angie took out her cell and was shooting live when a fluorescent light flickered on behind her.

"What do you think you're doing?" asked Lowell Felker. Standing beside him was Vance Dickason.

Angie stopped recording and shoved the phone into her handbag. She started for the door that led to the stairway.

Vance stepped in front of her.

"You're that tree-hugger," said Lowell. "The one always shooting off her mouth."

"Get out of my way," said Angie.

Lowell smiled. "We don't need to turn this into more than it is."

"I'll bet you don't."

"We know you're representing Todd Wendt. You've come in here illegally, snooping around to make some kind of case. We could get you disbarred for this, Miss. Prez."

"I'm leaving now, Felker, and neither you, or this pretty boy of yours is going to stop me."

As she moved once again toward the door, Vance grabbed her arms. Lowell stepped forward and the men overpowered her. She was strong, but no match for two of them. They dragged her down the hall and into Lowell's office. They had just crossed the threshold when Vance went to yank the cell phone from Angie's hand. She struggled and the phone dropped to the floor, Vance scrambling after it. Lowell lost his grip and Angie swung, catching him on the temple which clearly stunned him. Now in front of him, she kicked him mightily in the groin. Lowell's face went crimson and she kicked again, doubling him over.

Angie turned and started out of the office. Vance grabbed her and as they grappled, Lowell, enraged and gasping in pain, staggered over to his desk and grabbed the heavy, glass paperweight his wife had sent him. It filled his hand as he rushed forward and swung his arm in a powerful downward arc, catching Angie on the back of her skull; the impact so hard that the globe cracked. Angie fell sideways without a sound, just a surprised gust of breath as she collapsed on the floor.

Vance bent over her. She was on her side and he rolled her toward him. Blood was oozing from Angie's scalp, her eyes rolled up so far you could see only the very bottoms of her pupils. She wasn't moving as she made a few labored noises.

"My God, what did you do?" uttered Vance.

"We couldn't let her out of here."

Vance bent in even closer as Lowell said, "What's she saying? Is she saying anything?"

Vance looked up. "Boss, she isn't even breathing."

* * *

Lowell told Vance to call off that night's test and everyone went home with only the message that they would need to reschedule. The two of them sat up in Lowell's office, sipping Maker's until it finally grew so late that some kind of action could no longer be put off.

At four-twenty, Vance retrieved a dolly from the yard and brought it up on the elevator to the second floor. On top was an oversized burlap bag. Vance rolled the dolly down the hallway to Lowell's office as Lowell looked on, stunned, distressed and fairly intoxicated.

He held the bag open on the floor while Vance pulled Angie's lifeless body into it.

"When we get out there, you're gonna have to operate the lift," Vance told him.

In the yard, Lowell climbed onto the seat of one of the fork lifts and activated the engine. He fastened the forks onto both sides of the burlap bag and it ascended to the opening at the top of the twelve foot kiln. Then he released the hideous cargo.

Vance flung Angie's leather shoulder bag, her computer and cell phone inside, into the gaping space. Then he flipped the switch and Angie Prez's human remains were liquefied, to be ultimately covered with a few tons of cement.

* * *

In the pre-dawn darkness, Lowell followed Vance, who was at the wheel of Angie's Subaru, down Highway 38 for ten miles, to the turn for Knuckle Canyon which wove up into the mountains. They ascended steadily, starting at just over five thousand feet, winding upwards until, after twenty minutes, they were at an elevation of around eighty-five hundred. The road turned to a dirt path. After about a mile, Vance stopped the Subaru and hopped out. Lowell rolled down the window as Vance approached.

"Just wait here," Vance told him, "and I'll drive the car further in."

As Lowell waited, his breathing was shallow and there was tightness across his chest. This was bad, as bad as it could get. He'd seen all those shows on cable, the ones where seemingly ordinary people were caught on camera, discussing a contract murder with an undercover FBI man. He wasn't a murderer, it had been accident. The crazy bitch had no business snooping around. He nearly jumped out of his skin as Vance tapped on the passenger window. Lowell hit the button and the lock clicked open.

"If we're lucky," said Vance, "no one will come across it for at least a few days. You need me to drive?"

"No, I got it."

Lowell shoved the car into drive and swung the Escalade around. The two of them barely spoke all the way back to Lynton.

CHAPTER 27

Todd was in no hurry to get a car. Every place he wanted or needed to go – the grocery store, the pharmacy, the Wagging Tail or Ossies Blues n' Brew – was within walking distance. He also began taking walks for the pleasure of it and most often found himself walking south, crossing the wooden bridge above the south fork of the river and into Burnham Park. He'd pass through the park, into an open space that led to a trail, then a pleasant back road with a succession of residences, mostly small farms. Eventually that road became uninhabited, by humans and farm animals anyway, and he could walk for a long time and not encounter any people on foot or cycle or driving along the road.

What he did notice were birds, for which he was experiencing a growing curiosity. At first, he would spot a bird, study it as closely as possible and, when he returned to his place, try to find it online among the pictures and descriptions. He bought a pair of binoculars and a .35 millimeter camera and now his sightings could be more effectively documented. Only a few times was he unable to match what he'd seen and photographed with an identified species. He was growing familiar with not only the range and variation of the local bird population but which species were rare and which were well represented. He saw plenty of red-winged blackbirds and these were his day-to-day favorites. One day he snapped an amazing picture of a golden eagle, perched regally upon a telephone wire.

After one of these walks, reading a book he'd picked up at a local antique store called *Birds of Colorado,* he was startled by a sharp knock on his door. It was the first time anyone had called on him except for his landlady, Mrs. Winthrop.

Todd opened the door to a pair of serious looking guys in suits. One was around fifty, and introduced himself as Detective Laurie; the other, named Nieman, looked twenty years younger.

Laurie was medium height and stocky with thinning hair. Nieman was tall and sandy-haired and looked like somebody who'd moved to Colorado to be close to the slopes. Todd let them inside, freshly aware it was set up for a single person. He grabbed the lone wooden chair from the kitchen table and seated himself on the sofa beside Nieman.

"You're not the easiest man to locate," said Laurie. "Facing charges, yet you didn't file a change of address with the township."

"I didn't know I had to," said Todd.

"Well, your lawyer should have told you. By the way, when was the last time you spoke with Angela Prez?"

Todd involuntarily shifted his weight. "Early last week."

"That's when you fired her, right?" asked Nieman. "What was the reason for that?"

"She resigned. It wasn't because of any disagreement."

"He didn't ask what it *wasn't* about," said Laurie. "He asked what was the *reason*."

Todd's discomfort was growing. "I'd feel better about answering questions if I had an attorney present."

"You have a new attorney?" Laurie said with a smirk. "You replaced Ms. Prez already?"

"Like I told you, it was her decision. Ask Angie and she'll substantiate that."

Nieman offered a tight smile. "Angie Prez isn't talking. Her assistant reported her missing yesterday, and nobody's seen her since Friday."

Todd took that in, aware that both cops were studying him.

"Look, this is probably nothing." Laurie said. "Maybe Ms. Prez took a sudden trip, a family emergency or something. Maybe she just needed a few days to herself. But we're going to keep trying to find her and if she doesn't turn up, we'll be talking to you again. Since it seems like you want to be careful about what you tell us, then yeah, you might want to have your attorney with you."

"Your *new* attorney," said Nieman.

* * *

Todd went to Ossie's that night and drank more than his usual amount of ebony ale. Ossie was behind the bar, informally supervising a new female bartender. "I got a fresh batch of chili in the kitchen, Todd. Sure you don't want any?"

Todd shook his head.

Ossie leaned in close. "The cops talked to you today?"

Todd looked up like he hadn't heard him right, then took a deep breath. "How do you know that?"

"Because they talked to me. They're talking to everybody who knew Angie. She's the only person I know who works harder than I do. Married to her job. She wouldn't go missing unless she was in real trouble. What do you think's going on, Todd?"

"I wish I knew. But I have a bad feeling about it."

Ossie leaned in closer, all but whispering in Todd's ear. "Look, we never talked about it, because I had the sense you didn't want to, and it wasn't my place to bring it up. But I know you were set up, Todd. Angie told me that herself, and she told me who was behind it."

Todd didn't reply.

"If you have any idea what kind of danger she might have put herself in, you need to come out with it now."

Todd took another moment. "What you're saying is odd because Angie told me she didn't feel like she could help me."

Ossie pushed back from the bar. "That's not Angie. That's giving up, and that woman has never given up on anything in her life. I think Angie felt you were on to something and decided to follow up on her own. I just hope to God she didn't get herself hurt or even worse."

CHAPTER 28

Iris had done all she could, using her hand, her mouth, but she couldn't get Lowell to respond. "Is there still some KY in the bathroom cabinet?" she asked.

Lowell, lying on his back, uttered, "Let's just leave it alone for now."

Iris raised up on one elbow and looked at him. "What's goin' on with you, darlin'? I never thought I'd see the day when you wouldn't be..." She laughed. "You know, up for it. Ain't me, is it?"

Lowell reached out and pulled her to him. "I just got a lot on my mind." From down the hall came the strains of 'I'm So Lonesome I Could Cry' and Lowell flung aside the covers. "I'd better pick that up."

He threw on his robe and headed toward the chiming sound. Lowell stepped into his den-office, closed the door and lifted his cell from the desk. "Hello, Vance."

"Where you been, boss?"

"Just at home."

"I don't know how good it looks, you not coming in to the office. We don't want people to start asking questions."

"I just need a little time to pull it together."

"This Lynton cop, Cinda Rigg, keeps calling you at the plant."

Lowell flinched in response. "What do you think she wants?"

"I don't know but I think you'd better talk to her."

A long moment. "You don't think it's about... you know, that last night we were there."

"I hope not, but you need to deal with it, boss."

* * *

The fact that Lowell Felker ran the Mentex plant and that his beautiful stallion had been viciously attacked was not lost upon Officer Cinda Rigg, Wolfpaw's warning echoing in her mind. She had special knowledge, she felt, and with that came responsibility. That was why, after much soul searching, she'd been calling Felker's office to request a meeting. When he finally returned her call, he suggested they meet at The Wagging Tail.

He was already seated when she arrived, and she felt relieved that it was in the back, out of earshot of other patrons. He stood as she approached. They got themselves coffee and shared some inconsequential exchanges. Then Cinda said, "How've you been doing since losing your horse?"

"I got to admit," Lowell said, "I feel kind of bad to have been so emotional that day. Things don't usually hit me like that."

"No need to apologize for a genuine human reaction."

"You say it was a lion. I've seen tracks but never actually laid eyes on one."

Cinda took a breath. What she was doing was risky but she held on to the fact that he appeared so vulnerable in that pasture that perhaps he would hear her out. She spun the speech she'd been running through her head, trying to sound as rational as possible. But there was no getting around the main point of it. Something was causing the animals in the region to become dangerously aggressive. She referenced the stalking of Todd Wendt, the ravaging of the grave of Elias Howard Lynton, hordes of deer blocking the highway, the death of Lowell's own stallion. "Do you notice something about all of those incidents?"

Lowell looked at her with a decidedly neutral expression. "Go ahead and tell me."

"They all have to do with Mentex."

"With Mentex," he said. "You're all too familiar with Todd Wendt's situation, and he no longer works at Mentex. And what does Elias Howard Lynton, dead as Julius Caesar, have to do with *Mentex*?"

"There's a statue of him outside the facility, isn't there?"

"So what."

"And those deer lying down, that caused you to cancel the Mentex sponored music fest…"

It had all made sense when Cinda was turning it over in her mind, but presenting it to a virtual stranger, she felt like a madwoman. But there was no backing off now. "I think there's something going on at the plant that's causing the animals to react. And if it doesn't change, I'm afraid this is only the beginning."

Lowell looked down at his half-filled cup of coffee. It took him a long moment to return his gaze to Cinda. "Officer Rigg, I'm sure it was difficult for you to come in here with this kind of… theory you have. All I can tell you, there's nobody who knows more about what's taking place at the plant than I do. Whatever's going on with these animals has nothing to do with Mentex. And if you don't mind me saying it, I think you could use some time off or something. This job of yours seems to be getting to you."

* * *

Pinball Alley was a small but well stocked establishment on North Center Street. There weren't hoards of pinball enthusiasts but there were enough who came, not only from Denver, but, thanks to enthusiastic postings on the Internet, from as far away as Kansas and Nebraska, Wyoming and New Mexico to play the two dozen machines crowded into the place.

The two rooms, one main room and an adjacent smaller one, were always pitch-black, except for the neon glow of the classic fifties and sixties machines. The owner, who lived in Boulder, kept the place open at irregular hours. Saturday afternoons were the most consistent and that's when Lowell and Vance chose to meet. The machines were packed so tight there was barely elbow room, so the bells and buzzers and glare actually supported a private conversation. Lowell was manning Bucking Bronco and Vance was bent over his favorite, Creature From the Black Lagoon.

"So that engineer, Donaldson, is threatening to leave the project," Lowell was saying. "He still insists the cement cracked and caused all that fog and doesn't want to drill at the plant anymore. I have to convince him we need one final test to see if the solution holds or not before we start drilling at the new site."

Vance kept the flippers going and the bells sounding without missing a beat. "I thought we needed that patch of land to be annexed first."

"I'm gonna need to work on Wiggins."

Vance's game lit up several shades of green. "Work on him, how? It might take more than dangling a bike race in front of him."

"As a last resort, I'll cut him in."

"You think that's what it's gonna take, boss?"

"We're running out of time and we need the sonofabitch." Hands on either side of the machine, Lowell swayed like he was piloting a ship through choppy waves. "I know I've been MIA but I'm ready to get back on everything. The first thing is that goofy Animal Control officer I met with. She's full of questions about Mentex and I don't want her poking around."

Lowell's silver ball slipped out of play. The cowboy who'd been riding the Brahma bull was flung off into the air and the machine went dark and silent.

CHAPTER 29

Cinda was cruising on South Center Street. How many times had she done this, glided by the Laundromat and the music store and the nail place? She was coming up on the Pump It Up, in the twenty-five mile per hour zone, where so many careless commuters and tourists were given a dose of township justice. It was a significant source of revenue; half the cars that passed were ten miles over: some, fifteen or twenty. Fish in a barrel. The Odd Fellows hall was on her right, beyond a row of shrubbery, between the highway and the frontage road where officers on traffic patrol would aim the speed gun, ease out, and activate the lights and siren.

She spotted Randall's cruiser pushing forward from the growth at the roadside before swinging into her lane, directly behind her. He kept the tail up for nearly a minute as she tracked him in the rear view mirror. It was dark, so she couldn't see his face. Had it been light, Cinda was convinced he would have been grinning; she'd have waved at him and he'd have swung around her to get on with whatever had brought him out of hiding.

Cinda heard herself gasp as the garish lights came on, red and blue, spinning and swirling. He didn't use the siren, but the lights were enough. Cinda realized from this perspective how effective they were. The driver was practically cowering by the time you strode up to demand license, registration and proof of insurance. *All right, whatever you're up to, I'll just play along.*

Cinda eased over to the shoulder and waited. She wasn't about to get out from behind the wheel. Maybe Randall had a message from Ry, or more to the point, from Dora, the retired woman she'd hired to sit through the nights. She hoped it wasn't an emergency; that everything was all right. She'd rolled down the window by the time Randall appeared, his face reflected in the probing, changing light.

With a blank expression, he said, "Get out of the car, please."

"What's up, Randall?"

"Get out of the car, officer."

"This is a joke, right? What the hell's going on?"

"Don't make this any harder than it needs to be."

Cinda opened the door and eased herself out. It was warm outside, especially since she was in uniform. There was little or no traffic. That was good, as the sight of one cop pulling over another was likely not to pass unnoticed.

"What the hell are you doing, Randall?"

He had his flashlight out and on and was peering under the driver's seat. He leaned in even further and came up with something. Once he was fully turned and facing her, Cinda could see that it appeared to be a fifth of alcohol.

"And just what is that?"

"You know damn well what it is, Cinda. It's yours and you hid it there." Randall's youthful face looked surreal in the still twirling lights. "How could you do this, after I went to bat for you like I did?"

"How could I do *what*?"

"I covered for you once, but not this time. I got my own career to think about."

Cinda took a breath. She wanted him to be kidding but could tell this wasn't going to turn around. "This is ridiculous. Somebody put that there."

Randall shook his head. "It's your cruiser, Cinda. Nobody else has access."

A moment passed before he said, "This is an unsealed container. We can't be out here enforcing laws knowing that an officer-on-duty is breaking them."

Cinda felt a wave of emotion pass through her.

"Meet me back at the station."

When Cinda finally spoke, it seemed her own voice held some kind of weird echo.

"That isn't mine, Randall. Maker's Mark, isn't it? I don't even like whiskey."

* * *

There were half-a-dozen patrons in Valmont's All-night Eatery. Lowell and Vance were in a corner booth. Lowell was drinking coffee and had a blueberry muffin in front of him but hadn't touched it. Vance was digging into the a.m. special: a slab of ham, creamed corn, sweet potato and a buttermilk biscuit.

Lowell leaned forward. "Prez has been declared missing but they can't find her. Without a body, the case stays open. Cops don't like that. They like to wrap things up."

"They're never gonna come up with a body, we both know that."

"We know what a problem our friend from Mentex headquarters has been for us. For all we know, Prez told him she was coming to the plant to investigate and he's just waiting to use it against us in his trial. Before, this was a project but now we're fighting for our lives."

Vance chewed on a slice of ham, then took a sip of orange juice.

"What've you got in mind, boss?"

"The cops think Wendt is a sex offender. That's what he's charged with. And now his attorney, his *female* attorney is missing... Maybe the cops figure he admitted his crime and she bailed and he needed her out of the way. Maybe he killed Prez, then got rid of her body up in the mountains. Maybe he's so screwed up, his next move is to go up there somewhere and off himself."

The younger man leaned back, his eyes darting around the near-empty restaurant.

"Vance, we didn't mean for it to happen, but somebody got killed and we both were there and in the eyes of the law, that makes us killers."

Vance, in a soft voice said, "I'm no killer."

Lowell's voice was even softer. "I'm no killer either, Vance... That doesn't mean somebody doesn't need to be killed."

CHAPTER 30

He was being guided by the pits that bordered either side of his eyes, determining the temperature and indicating what was up ahead. He was winding through the dirt and the grass, all four feet of him. He felt at the top of his power, having three pairs of fangs that replaced the ones he had recently shed. He'd grown a new rattler, having shed the other a few weeks before. His skin was fresh and new too, the diamond pattern adorning his back.

Still light out, he would slip in and find the right spot to hide until the moment he'd be forced to reveal himself. He would rise up and look into the face, the one revealed to him that day the leader attacked the big white. Would he survive his mission? Maybe not, but it had been a good life. Twenty summers he had lived. He loved the rocks and sand and the sweetness of the air. He felt ready for a good long sleep. But this had to be done and he was the one chosen to do it.

Maybe ten yards away now, he would wait until the door lifted open to allow one of the swift, four-legged cages to ease out, then he would slip into the usually dark space. There was another door leading into where the big, light-haired human lived, the one most responsible for sending the poison into the sky. Once inside, he would cling to the corners until he could determine when to slink unobserved and rise up at the right moment.

* * *

Cinda's dismissal was page one of the Lynton Weekly Record: *Township Officer Fired for Open Container.*

Of course she'd been set up. Randall was only part of it. This had to be Felker.

Cinda needed to work and the only job she'd ever had in

Lynton was the one she'd just lost. When she applied at the tree nursery and the hardware store and at Monroe's Auto Parts, she encountered a chill. Cinda couldn't leave Colorado even if she wanted to because of her divorce decree. Plus, Ry's whole world was in Lynton: school, friends, everything. She had enough to stay afloat for a couple of months, but needed a job and was being frozen out.

Totally at loose ends one night – Ry was with his father – Cinda found herself at the bar at Ossie's, the bottles gleaming, murmuring to her. *Pick me, pick me. I'm your friend, pick me.*

"What'll it be, sis?"

Cinda looked at a twenty-something female bartender she'd never seen before. "Um, what kinds of soft drinks do you have?"

"Coke products, plus some awesome draft root beer... iced tea, lemonade."

"Iced tea, I guess, with lemon."

Cinda looked around and noticed what she had not taken in before. Lowell Felker sat in a corner booth, the glass in front of him filled with something amber, over ice.

"Excuse me," said Cinda to the bartender. "That guy over there in the corner. Would you mind telling me what he's drinking?"

"You want to buy Lowell a drink? The drinks are usually on him."

"No, no... I'm just curious."

"Maker's Mark. What Lowell always drinks."

A feeling rushed through Cinda. Felker had even sent his own malicious signal.

She dashed out the open doorway, rushed down the stairs and stepped out into the evening. Leaning against the brick wall, she tried to catch her breath. She'd bought some cigarettes during her last stop at the Pump-it-Up, Spirit Menthols. Hands trembling, she reached into her bag and pulled out the dark green pack. She took hold of one and yanked it out. Did she still have those matches? Yes, there they were. She struck one and held it to the tip, then inhaled deeply. A ridiculous habit, but so was caffeine, of which she'd tripled her intake since becoming unemployed. Cinda knew she was an addict; she just needed to pick her poisons with care.

She became aware of a guy standing in front of her. Late fifties, early sixties, gray hair. Some kind of loose Hawaiian shirt. He was right in her face, booze on his breath. "Don't remember me do you?"

"Why should I remember you?"

"I'm Roger Blankenship. You gave me a ticket. Forty-eight in that goddamn twenty-five."

"Get to the point."

"*Points.* I was carrying points on my license and that put me over. Couldn't drive for six months; had to shop for new insurance and it didn't come cheap."

"I don't make the laws, mister."

"Where the hell you from, anyway?"

"None of your—"

"Canned your ass, didn't they? Drinking on the job, you ought to be ashamed of yourself." He turned to go back inside. Over his shoulder he said, "This is a small town with a long memory. Good luck finding work here again."

Cinda closed her eyes. If she'd ever felt this lost and miserable, she couldn't remember when. Then she sensed that once again she was no longer alone. She opened her eyes and Todd Wendt was standing there, holding out a tall glass of iced tea.

"You left this inside."

Cinda awkwardly took the glass from him. "I'm not a cop anymore. Suppose you heard about that."

"Yeah, they got the word out fast." They stood there a moment, then Todd said, "Why don't we go back in? I'd like to hear what you did to Felker to make him come after you."

* * *

As Lonnie and SB walked along the dense overgrown riverbank, they came across a campsite in a tight clearing. Lonnie switched on his flashlight and approached the small tent, cautiously checking it out.

"C'mon, I thought you didn't want to be late," said SB.

Lonnie was smirking when he came back.

"Remember that spooky bastard's trailer we broke into last year? The one who walked by that night we got busted at the Chink Palace. I'll bet that sonofabitch *did* turn us in. That's some of his same crummy stuff in that tent. Not a goddamn thing worth taking, remember? Like that shitty cup, all dented and crumpled up. That creep must be homeless now. I don't like him floating around here."

They walked until they reached the gravel path that led into Juniper Park, then walked to the playground where Vance Dickason said they'd meet. Lonnie settled into a swing while SB sat in the sand beside the monkey bars. There was a wash of moonlight and the murmur of the river rushing over the rocks at the base of the mountain. Five minutes later, a pair of headlights probed toward them in the darkness.

Vance was driving and he and Lowell climbed out, Lowell taking the lead. "Thanks for showing up, boys."

"Good to see you, Mr. Felker."

Lonnie was on his feet, SB back and to the side. Lowell trained his attention on Lonnie. "How would you fellas like to make some money?"

"Sure," said Lonnie. "So long as it's *serious* money."

"Serious money for serious work. Much more serious than that little problem you took care of for me at the Cowpoke. Just one guy, but he doesn't get up this time. Stays down and goes under. It'll look like a robbery gone bad. We'll give you all the details the night before it happens."

"So how much you willing to pay?" sneered Lonnie.

Lowell looked at Vance who was already peeling off bills. "Here's some upfront earnest money. There'll be more when the work's done. You get caught, you'll be twisting in the wind by yourselves."

Lonnie laughed, taking the cash. "We get caught, that means we fucked up."

Lowell laughed himself. "That's right. So don't fuck up."

Lowell held out his hand and Lonnie awkwardly shook it, then Lowell and Vance headed back to the Escalade.

When Vance turned over the engine, the lights came on and the scene was once again cast in the eerie light.

"You think we can count on them, boss?"

Lowell chuckled. "Like I told you – green as hell, but *mean* as hell."

* * *

Fourteen-year-old Barry Quinn felt rehearsal was going really smooth. Iris had wanted to go over the material they'd be recording tomorrow. They'd be cutting at a cool studio up in the mountains and Barry was finding he loved recording even more than playing live.

Barry had picked up the guitar at seven and it always felt like the easiest, most natural thing he'd ever done. He could play acoustic and electric with equal skill; had breezed through folk and bluegrass, blues and rock and now what he focused on when playing solo was jazz. He hoped to go to Berkeley School of Music in Boston and make a career out of his natural passion.

Barry could hear Iris in the kitchen whipping up some food. They'd skipped dinner, having started late and now the musicians were hungry. After eating, Iris would decide whether they should go through everything one more time or knock off for tomorrow's ten a.m. session. Barry was alone in the huge front room, going over the opening riff he wanted to get just right. After a few runs, he settled his beloved Collings into its open case and was ready for a well-earned meal. Not knowing whether or not they were done for the night, he left the case open.

* * *

Besides the Pump It Up, there was one other Lynton establishment that stayed open around the clock – that is, if you were a member and knew the combination to open the front door. Lynton 24-7 Fitness was owned by Mattie Kerrigan, who also taught most of the classes. She retained ownership after an extremely contentious divorce from Devon Antwerp, the most active accountant in Lynton.

The facility was modest but it was the only game in town. Dale Wiggins had joined the previous October to train on one of the two stationary bikes during the winter months. But he'd found that pedaling in an unchanging space after years of gliding along the highways and back roads and trails was just too boring. Instead, he clocked most of his time on the treadmill which, for some reason unknown to him, didn't have quite the same dulling effect.

Dale liked going at night, preferably the middle of the night, when there was a ninety-plus percent chance that he'd be the only one present. He was on the treadmill at two-thirty a.m. when Lowell Felker, as arranged, walked in. In advance of Lowell's arrival Dale had tuned the sound system to KFLT, the rock station out of Boulder. The two shared a few meaningless exchanges as Lowell stepped on the adjacent treadmill, Dale keeping a 4.2 pace while Lowell lagged with a more conservative 3.5.

"We all could use more exercise," said Dale, "but something tells me that's not why you wanted to talk."

"I know you did your homework before taking office. But I'm gonna tell you something your late predecessor shared with me. Parts of Lynton never became incorporated. Unlike Mentex, some aren't even part of Boulder County and, as far as zoning goes, don't have to answer to squat. Hell, it's the Wild West."

There was the sound of the dual treadmills, humming along with an REM cut from the nineties.

"Since this is headed somewhere, why don't we just get to it?"

Lowell was breathing a bit deeper from his steady pace. He hit the red button and the conveyer belt slowed and then stopped. He stepped off, a towel around his neck, yanked it off and swept his forehead.

Taking the cue, Dale stopped his machine as well.

There was a wooden bench against the far wall and Lowell led the way for them to sit. Dale settled in beside him.

"There's somebody I want you to meet. I can't tell you much about it except that you're going to want to hear what he has to say. It could turn out to be... life-changing."

"Something tells me this isn't about a bike race."

Lowell smiled. "Like I said, life-changing."

* * *

Barry and Iris were in the control room sipping coffee. Gus, the engineer, was out in the room resetting the microphones.

"What are we doing first?" asked Barry.

"Let's start with Head Over Heels," said Iris.

She seemed excited but relaxed. Barry felt it would be a great session. "You want electric or acoustic?"

"Let's lay acoustic for the rhythm track and you can overdub the lead on your Strat."

"Got it," said Barry.

Iris left the control room and Barry stepped over and,

balanced on one knee, flipped open the brass locks on his hard-shell case. The guitar had felt a little heavier the previous night when they'd knocked off after a long meal, Barry had written it off to feeling tired.

As he lifted the guitar, he heard something knock around inside it and his first thought was that the pick-up had become dislodged. He lay the guitar across his lap and leaned forward, peering into the sound hole. He heard an odd shaking. Barry was strangely mesmerized as the strings were forced apart and then, like a jack-in-the-box, a triangular head had uncoiled itself, looking Barry directly in the face. As Barry's arms went up defensively, there was a thrashing motion as though a whip had been slung, and the rattler snapped its fangs and venom into Barry's left forearm.

Barry tried to rise only to collapse as the rattler drew back, then slithered onto the floor toward the open door.

CHAPTER 31

Wolfpaw was standing in the graveyard at the north edge of Lynton, waiting for the lion. He'd told the red-tailed hawk to go to the mountains and get him, as Wolfpaw was as angry as he'd ever been. He'd seen that Quinn kid play more than once at those mini-concerts the town would hold in the park. The boy had been gifted, brilliant, and now his arm had been amputated and he'd never play guitar again.

Scanning the open silver-blue sky, Wolfpaw spotted the hawk descending. He remained still as a statue as the hawk swooped onto his shoulder, fluttering its wings before settling. Now Wolfpaw caught a glint in the darkness and those eyes were coming right toward him. The lion was in no hurry, loping rather than bounding, stopping right in front of Wolfpaw before gazing up, waiting. Wolfpaw's river of emotions was running through him. He would try to crystalize his thoughts, keep them straight and true.

"That boy who was attacked was innocent. Now he has to go through life as a half-person. I have done what I can for you. I want nothing more to do with this place. It has become sick with evil. I am leaving for good at dawn but there is someone I want to point out before I go. He was with them but is no longer. He may even be trying to help. I will show him to you and ask for your promise that no harm come to him or anyone else who is not part of the poison. There has been enough blood. I want your promise that you will kill no humans in the short time I remain here. After I am gone tomorrow, do as you wish."

As the hawk pushed off him, Wolfpaw felt a weight much greater than that leave his body. He turned and headed south toward town. The lion stood looking at him, then sullenly followed.

Todd couldn't sleep. His temples were throbbing and it felt like a headache was coming on. He got out of bed and went into the bathroom to the medicine cabinet. Alka Seltzer, Listerine and ah, a bottle of Anacin, but only one lone, white tablet at the bottom. He needed at least two, maybe three. He wasn't too thrilled about going out in the middle of the night. The only place open was the Pump It Up, out on Highway 38.

Todd stepped onto the outside landing. A few scattered lights were glowing. There appeared to be a thin coat of condensation from the heat on every surface. He walked out into the night, crossed Business 38, passing the little park with the town center and the band shell. There was a Coke machine outside the center and something about its red glow was soothing to Todd. He found himself wondering if the machine dispensed twelve-ounce aluminum cans or twenty-ounce plastic bottles, whether it cost a buck, a buck twenty-five or a buck-fifty. Did it demand exact change? Then he caught himself and laughed. Who cared, what on earth did it matter?

In what seemed like no time at all, he was at the Pump It Up, its white neon glowing defiantly against the night. He'd been there late before, but never this late. Two women traded the night shift. One was quite overweight and Todd recalled a time she'd left the counter to check some item on the shelf and came back to the register breathing noticeably harder than before. The other woman was tall, surely over six feet, and wore her rust-shaded hair in a way that resembled a bird house perched atop her head. As skinny as she was tall, her age was not easily determined. She could have been thirty, could have been sixty. She was at the counter when Todd entered.

He went to the spot where they kept the mini-packs of aspirin and sundries. There was no Anacin, but there was Excedrin, his second choice. It had previously been his pain-drug of preference, until he read about its effect on the liver, so he switched to Anacin, which had caffeine but not the other multi-lettered stuff. Anacin, however, was harder to find, especially in a place of limited selections.

"That'll be two-twenty-five," said the woman behind the counter. She wore a green blouse with a name tag pinned to the front but the space where the name would appear was blank. As she was ringing him up, Todd's eyes fell to a display of Marlboro cigarettes in all of their various machinations: Lights, 100s, Menthols, Ultra Lights, Reds... "Wow," he said, almost to himself. "How many different kinds of Marlboros are there?"

The woman looked at him through her silver rimmed glasses. "I never counted them, mister. Do you want a pack?"

"No, I don't smoke."

"Then what the hell do you care?" She handed him his change.

Todd left her to her cash register and expansive display.

Outside, to the right of the station, where the lights from the pumps and the service center were dim, his knees buckled from a blow to the middle of his back.

More blows to his ribs as he curled up on his side. No other sound, except the thud of heavy boots pounding his bones. He heard himself groan, then a harsh male voice said, "C'mon, grab hold of his legs."

"Think he'll stay down?" Another male voice.

"He'll stay down."

Todd was kicked again, every ounce of breath going out of him. Then some rush of energy, some desperate sense of survival swept up inside from his gut to his chest, spreading to his arms and shoulders. He leaped up and threw a right and met nothing but air, then followed with a left that connected with something hard and sharp and he heard an astonished groan.

"Sonofabitch, get hold of his arms."

Todd glimpsed the two of them, one short and one tall, both wearing dark ski masks. After the surge of strength, he now felt close to blacking out. They grabbed him again and he was dragged from the shadows alongside the Pump It Up. He wondered if that nameless clerk inside would glimpse what was happening, but that hope flew away. There was one on each side of him and he knew that even if he tried to fight back, he'd extinguished what force he had in him.

"Where we taking him?" asked the bigger one on his right.

"Sonofabitch broke my tooth. Lay him flat."

Todd was shoved face down, nose pressed into the pavement.

"Give me the rope."

Todd's hands were yanked behind his back and swiftly secured.

"Now his legs, C'mon."

Todd tried to struggle but it was no use, tried to cry out but what voice he had couldn't rise up through his throat.

An odd silence had fallen over everything. Off to Todd's left came a grating, guttural sound, like two sheets of sandpaper being slowly rubbed together.

"What the hell was that?" one his attackers uttered.

"We need to get out of here."

Todd struggled with what little he had left but was effectively hog-tied.

"Shouldn't we throw him in the trunk?"

"No, we need to go, right now."

There was no sound beyond their boots receding on the pavement. Then an engine fired up, followed by a car speeding away.

Todd lay there. His hands were bound too tight, he couldn't get them free. His legs were tied securely. He tried to roll, but couldn't, his body too weak to respond.

He lifted his head. A pair of headlights, and the sound of a much bigger engine slowing down, most likely a truck.

He felt something beside him, then the sensation of heat and air pushing toward him. Something took hold of the rope securing his hands, tugging at it forcefully until they were free. Then he became aware that the same presence was vigorously loosening the pair of ropes binding his legs.

Todd lay with his face to the ground for what seemed like a very long time.

A voice called out to him. "Mister, are you okay?"

Todd tried to respond but produced only a weak utterance.

After a moment, he was aware of the dim figure of a man.

"Why the hell were you tied up like that?"

"Somebody jumped me, attacked me."

The voice was incredulous. "I figured you'd be all chewed up. Hell, man, you had a mountain lion all over you..."

CHAPTER 32

Lonnie and SB ditched their stolen car on a leafy side street, crossed the highway headed south, then turned west and ran along the river, winded from the failed attack and from making their escape.

As they neared the bridge, *their* bridge, the one that had given their club its name, Lonny said, "My tooth's cracked. This is a fucking mess. Didn't you see that spook watching us?"

"What the hell are you talking about?"

"That spooky bastard. The one whose tent's pitched by the river. Sonofabitch was watching the whole time."

"You musta' been seeing things."

"While you was tying that bitch up, I yanked off my mask to spit some blood. I looked over and saw these gleamy eyes, staring at us from the brush." Lonnie pulled out the .22. "He saw me, plain as day. The dude ratted us out for the Chink Place and that was nothing. We need to waste that old coot off before he gabs to somebody."

"Waste him when?"

"Now, tonight. Go to his campsite and wait till he shows. Then we need to waste him. He's some kind of witch doctor or some shit. We can't afford to have him floating around here."

SB nodded and Lonnie was relieved he didn't have to tell him the other part, because it was just too weird. Yes, he'd seen that old coot but those weren't the eyes he'd looked into. The eyes he'd looked into weren't human, they were beast eyes, the eyes of a lion, standing right beside the old coot, looking like it was ready to come after them and tear out their throats.

But why hadn't it?

* * *

Todd remained conscious the whole time but the pain was incredible. He was wheeled through the emergency room at Boulder County Hospital and given a series of x-rays to determine whether he was bleeding internally. It appeared he wasn't, although they ordered an MRI for first thing in the morning. They hooked him up to a morphine drip to ease the pain, which helped but, at first, made him sick. The physician on duty gave him something further to sleep but even with that it took Todd a while to shut down.

The next day, in and out of sleep, he was relieved to learn that nothing was broken, no internal bleeding. The attack had been swift and brutal and they clearly weren't after money but wanted him maimed or dead. *Lowell Felker* wanted him dead and was likely behind Angie Prez's disappearance and even her death. Whatever Felker was up to had to be bigger than Todd ever imagined... Big enough to kill for. And was it a lion who freed up his hands? That was the part Todd couldn't wrap his mind around. He was caught up in something so bizarre, he didn't want it to push him over what rational bearings he had left.

He saw a figure at the side of his bed, a woman. His brain was fuzzy and he didn't immediately recognize her. She was wearing some kind of uniform. Then she smiled and said in her Auckland accent, "I hear you're being released tomorrow."

Todd managed to smile back. His lips moved but nothing came out.

"How do you feel?"

"Like hell." There was a moment, then Todd managed, "What are you doing here, Cinda?"

"I got a job working security in the emergency room, the night shift. I was on duty when they brought you in."

"So outside of Lynton, you're still employable."

Cinda reached down and took Todd's hand. "I don't think you should be alone."

Todd took a painful breath. "I don't think so either."

CHAPTER 33

Dwight Shevney loved the West. Originally from Saddle River, New Jersey, his great-grandfather had made two fortunes, one in rubber and one in petroleum. Dwight never had to work but did so nonetheless, concerning himself directly with the family's vast and far-flung holdings. "Any man who can't look after his own money, deserves what he gets," was a saying he was fond of.

Shevney attended Yale and the Wharton School, eventually settling in Jackson Hole, Wyoming, where the family vacationed when he was a boy. But the better part of his adult life was spent in the nation's capital, overseeing the lobbyists who advocated for his family's fortune. He'd never held office and never wanted to; politicians came and went, people who owed people like him favors.

Shevney first met Lowell Felker at a rodeo in Cheyenne several years before and liked his idea about burning tires for a fuel source. But that hadn't worked out, as then mayor of Lynton, Ned Haddock, folded like a squeezebox at the first whiff of controversy.

Felker's most recent scheme, providing the much-in-demand cement for fracking, would assure Felker's fortune, and surely enhance Shevney's. They'd agreed to meet at Haddocks' lodge-like compound in Jackson Hole. When Lowell and Vance, after being granted entry by security, pulled up in the Escalade, Dale Wiggins had yet to show.

"Just wait outside until the honorable mayor turns up," Lowell told Vance.

"Will do, boss."

Vance was as aware as Lowell that his previously limited stock had risen in their relationship. Even though he wouldn't be involved in the actual meeting, Vance knew so much, especially about the death of Angie Prez, that Lowell had to take him all the way along on a course that would set high school dropout Vance Dickason up for life.

Vance was thinking all this, feeling really good about everything, when Dale Wiggins arrived in his funky Pathfinder. Vance greeted the mayor and walked him to the door, telling him to go right on in.

Dale walked through a large living room and kept moving forward until he heard a set of voices. He turned left and entered a smaller but by no means small room to his left.

"Ah, the mayor's here," Lowell's voice boomed.

Lowell introduced Dale to Dwight Shevney, who, in his sixties, with close-cropped white hair, sat smiling at the end of the long table. Dale was thrown back a step. Shevney's name was synonymous with fracking, had been the one most responsible for introducing it to Wyoming where whole communities had their natural resources infused with gas and chemicals. Dale had seen interviews Shevney had given on Fox News and CNN. Both Shevney and Lowell were dressed as though they were attending some parody of a western cookout. Dale had blue jeans above his usual sandals and a CU Buffs t-shirt.

"I see you got all spruced up for us," said Lowell.

Shevney laughed. "Whatcha' drinkin'?"

"How about some water?" said Dale.

"We can manage that." Shevney called over to a middle-aged guy standing at a bar in the corner of the room. "Fergie, get the mayor some water." He turned again to Dale. "You sure you don't wanna go crazy, cranberry juice or something?"

"Water's fine," said Dale.

He glanced around the room. Mounted on every wall were animal heads, their eyes gazing out at nothing. On one wall were an elk and a deer. On another, a moose and a mountain goat. He turned, and behind him, a fox and coyote. Facing him were a wolf and a bobcat.

"Are all those real?" asked Dale, as the barman handed him the water in a plastic bottle.

"What do you mean?" said Shevney.

"The heads, those are real animals?"

Shevney laughed. "Were at one time."

"How'd you get them?" asked Dale.

Shevney glanced at Lowell. "I shot them, what the hell do you think?"

"You shot a bobcat?"

"I shot every blessed one of them. Bunch of others, too. Started pretty soon after I moved west. Hell, you gotta let these creatures know who's in charge out here."

Dale pulled out a chair and sat.

It didn't take long before Shevney got them down to business. At his urging, Lowell laid it all out for Dale, what was expected of him once everything was in place. Dale Wiggins, committed cyclist and espoused environmentalist, was to be a key player in supplying cement to myriads of companies engaged in the controversial and risky process of bringing natural gas up from the ground. Mentex would remain under the county's jurisdiction, and Lowell's new venture, unincorporated and yet to be named, would be annexed as part of a new district that would come under the protective arm of the township. Once the arrangement was finalized, they would unveil the company to Lynton, to Boulder County, the state of Colorado, the essential players in Washington, and to international petroleum. If Dale had ever dreamed of being rich, it would far exceed those dreams.

When they looked to Dale for his response, his head was swimming. He took a moment, then said, "Respectfully, gentlemen, I think you're underestimating the public response to all this."

Lowell looked at Dale and said, "We'll be handling the county and the state and anything in Washington. You just need quash any local objections."

"If this is gonna work," Dale replied, "you need the town, and I mean the *whole* town, to buy in on it."

Lowell squinted as he peered back at him. "Buy in, *how*?"

"A ballot referendum."

Lowell leaned toward him. "A *vote,* is that what you're talking about?"

Shevney, who'd been looking hard at Dale, appeared to brighten a bit. "I think the mayor's on to something. We could be totally open about the new company, sell it to the town by telling them what new jobs it might mean for them, and hard sell the potential for revenues and growth."

Lowell shook his head, the redness in his face deepening. "It seems like a roll of the dice. You never know how people are going to react when you put something like this out to them."

Dale took a gulp of water. "There'll be plenty of dissention, but if people think the new plant is going to increase their personal fortunes, they might go for it."

"Plus," said Shevney, "there's something else you're not considering."

"What the hell's that, Dwight?" asked Lowell.

"We'll be the ones counting the votes."

* * *

Shevney's lodge could accommodate up to thirty guests. Dale Wiggins had a spacious pine paneled room upstairs, in the corner, with plenty of light. After their lunch meeting which included elk steaks and ale, Shevney made it clear they were all pretty much on their own until dinner when more business would be conducted.

Dale felt ill at ease. It was clear to him how big this venture was, how much power and money and influence was involved. Dealing with a small-time, small-town wrangler like Lowell

Felker, was one thing; climbing in bed with Dwight Shevney and everything he represented was more than he'd bargained for.

And now that he had some time and space to ponder it, he didn't care how much money was involved, Dale didn't want any part of it.

He was running through his mind the speech he'd make before leaving tomorrow: that they'd have to find somebody else.

Dale glanced over at his phone, which he'd placed next to his overnight bag. He'd give Lydia a call. He hadn't been so nice to her lately, had been distracted and impatient. He had the urge to babble about how beautiful it was up here and what an interesting time he was having, but really it was just to make contact, knowing she'd appreciate it, knowing it would make him feel... well, normal.

Dale was moving toward the phone when there was a light but firm rapping on the closed bedroom door. He went to open it.

A man stood there, sixty, maybe, with a craggy face and hair the bluish color of steel wool, one of Shevney's hired hands.

"Yes?" said Dale.

"Mr. Shevney's going shooting and would like you to accompany him."

"Shooting... when?"

"Now."

* * *

There was a clearing behind the lodge the size of a football field, acres of woods beyond it. Dale saw that Shevney was waiting with another man who looked somewhat younger than the one who'd summoned Dale from his quarters. Shevney had donned a beige jacket and matching cap, with baggy, olive pants tucked into what looked like a pair of ancient, reddish, riding boots.

"This is Marcel," Shevney told Dale. "He's deaf as a post but will act as spotter, his vision being extremely keen. I didn't get a weapon for you but it can be arranged if you like."

"No thanks, I didn't plan to be doing any shooting this weekend."

As Shevney walked toward the woods, he said, "I figured you weren't a hunter, Wiggins. And since you aren't, now probably isn't the time for you to be taking charge of a high-powered rifle. Me, I've been shooting since I was five. My father and grandfather insisted on it."

"Is there a lot of game out here?"

"Those woods and hills are stocked, the same way you'd stock a river with trout. Regional species mostly, that's what I shoot here. I still enjoy going to Africa once a year to bag some big game. Those trophies are all at my estate back East."

"I assume it's a lot different, shooting... bigger animals."

"Oh, hell yes. I shot an elephant when I was thirteen. My grandfather arranged the trip. Because I was a kid, I dreaded the thought of shooting something so huge and exotic. But when it came down to it, it was easy. Thrilling, in fact. The beast collapsed like a house being excavated."

They walked in silence for a moment. Marcel was up ahead, training a pair of field glasses on the dense trees.

"Why did you want me to come with you, sir?" Dale asked. "Not any of the others."

"Well, we're going to be doing some important work together and, while I know a lot about you, we've never had a face-to-face."

"You know a lot about me?"

Dale was aware that all he'd been doing was asking questions but now even those dissolved and he was simply listening, a sense of dread washing over him. Nearing the woods, Dale felt like his own footfalls were echoing inside the walls of his skull.

Shevney's eyes were trained ahead. "Do you remember the Golden Trust in Telluride?"

"I lived in Telluride, but I don't remember the Golden Trust."

"Well, you never had an account there. Back in those days you were with old, reliable Wells Fargo. But my family holds the majority of Golden Trust's forty-seven branches in Colorado. Small, but lucrative. Back when you were a fledging coke dealer, you did indeed oversee a transaction at the Telluride Golden Trust."

Dale felt frozen in his own footsteps, but kept moving forward. "I have no idea what you're talking about."

"When I ran my check, and believe me it was thorough as can be, we sifted the dirt regarding your history dispensing the devil's dandruff. Once we found that out, I demanded we look further because something took place in Telluride during the time you were there that remains something of a mystery."

Now they were in the woods, on a narrow trail. The light through the limbs and branches made the leaves appear phosphorous. Dale felt ghostly and disembodied as Shevney kept droning in a matter-of-fact tone that in no way suited the highly charged scenario.

"Evan Mattingly died in Telluride around that time. I'd known that kid since he'd run around like a banshee during Thanksgivings at Saddle River. Never cared much for him but the family is... *family*, you know? His dad and I roomed together at New Haven; were admitted to the same senior society, at the same time. In the investigation, it turned out one of Evan's last acts was to withdraw a wad of cash at two-fourteen in the morning from the Golden Trust ATM. He was found dead several hours later by one of the many local girls he'd been screwing. The autopsy revealed the stuff he'd snorted was cut with strychnine. What's the phrase, *stepped on*? The Mattinglys vowed if they ever found the dealer, they'd either have him killed or find a very tight cell and throw away the key."

Shevney halted for a moment, like he'd spotted something in the brush. Then he shook his head as if he'd been seeing things, and continued.

"You were questioned about it weren't you, Dale? There were plenty of cameras in front of the bank, even back then. And your car, a white 1991 Saab, Colorado License 646 TVS was one of the few that drove by around that time. Nobody saw you park; the bank cameras had Evan strolling up to the ATM on his own. But when I looked into your history and found you'd been questioned about being in proximity that night and that you'd left Telluride shortly after, never to return again, I started looking even further. A lot further, believe me, than the Telluride police and the CBI ever did. That's when I became acquainted with your coke dealing adventures."

"I had nothing to do with what you're accusing me of."

Shevney laughed. "Accusing is an interesting word. The word *using* is hidden in there at the end. I'm not accusing you, Dale, but I *am* using you. Because both you and I know that Evan Mattingly, the *late* Evan Mattingly, twenty-three years young, who was out there sniffing a few more wild oats before settling down to assume his rightful place among the family chemical fortune, got hold of some too-hot powder and that you're the one who sold it to him. No statute of limitations for the kind of charges you'd be facing and the current DA owes me a whole pocketful of favors."

Dale felt tightness in his chest that was rising to his throat. The door where he kept his rankest, darkest secret had been opened and there was nothing to do but let the vapors seep out and settle.

But Shevney was paying him no mind, his eyes and senses trained on Marcel, who had spotted something and was now pointing.

Spotting it himself, Shevney raised his rifle. A beige creature, clearly not a raccoon but the size of a large one, was loping in the brush, white mask-like stripes adorning its forehead. It stopped as though it sensed it was under threat. The animal rose on its hind legs, then took a step backward, at the same time baring its teeth and claws and emitting a hiss that was angry and defiant.

Shevney squeezed the trigger and Dale recoiled at the blast.

The beige form in the brush spurted blood from its eyes, ears and mouth, all at once, as it whirled backward, landing lifeless on the ground.

Silence for a moment, broken by Shevney's voice.

"Fine work, Marcel," he said, striding toward his kill. "Looks like we'll be serving badger kabob this evening."

CHAPTER 34

He had been searching for days. It was not a blind search, for the bird with wide wings had last seen their two-legged friend walking along the river. Now the friend was missing and the lion sensed he had been attacked like the other two-leg, maybe even later that same night.

At the riverbank, the lion could not keep himself from stretching down and tasting the water. It had been so harmed he could hardly swallow it. The air smelled harsh as well but here, in this spot, there was something else mixed with it. He smelled it more strongly as he made his way up the bank, to a spot where the damp, dark ground had been disturbed. It was what he did not want to find. When a two-leg was no longer drawing air, the other two-legs dug a hole and put the dead one in it, covering it with dirt.

He began clawing and digging, tossing the soil behind him and off to the side. His friend didn't deserve to be down there, eaten by the foul creatures who breathed underground. The lion knew he needed to hurry because the bright was pushing through and spreading from above. He didn't want to be here once it arrived but was grateful for it because then his friend would be out of the ground.

* * *

As she ran along the river, Cinda was thinking this was the first time in weeks she'd truly felt good. Ry was away, having gone with his father to Sacramento, to visit the paternal grannies and, although she missed him, she was relieved to be an adult on her own. *His father,* that's how she'd come to think of her ex. She didn't loathe Gordon, didn't even resent him. He'd simply become someone with whom she'd shared a bedroom and a few memorable conversations, who would show up periodically and disappear with her son for a pre-arranged amount of time.

Since her divorce, she hadn't experienced much in the way of romance. There was the guy she'd met online who claimed to be an architect, then moved out of state when he was offered a warehouse job at a Home Depot in Omaha. Then there was the guy she'd gone home with from a sports bar one night in Boulder, a coach from CU, rugby or soccer or something. He'd left her a note beside the empty fifth on his kitchen table: *feel free to make yourself breakfast.*

Cinda was pretty freaked out when she'd missed her next monthly. Although a false alarm, it would have been a kind of Immaculate Conception, as she didn't recall one thing about the end of the night, yet woke up alone in an unfamiliar bed, her clothes strewn about the bedroom.

That had been shortly before she began going to meetings.

But what about Todd Wendt, who'd been at her place for two nights now? They'd made meals together and watched films on Netflix. He was sleeping on the sofa in the tiny den off the kitchen. Nothing romantic had passed between them, nothing physical anyway. For one thing, Todd was clearly in pain from being attacked and Cinda had seen the dreadful bruises on his back. He was starting to get around better and she'd considered asking him if he wanted to go for a walk, then decided to wait and see if Todd suggested it himself. They were both aware that whoever attacked Todd was still out there, maybe even in close proximity.

The Boulder County Police questioned him in the hospital but Todd hadn't shared his suspicions as to who might have been behind his attack. Felker clearly had the Lynton police in his pocket, who knew what other authorities might have been bought off? Cinda had already decided that any outing she and Todd might take would include her Charter Arms .38.

It was a little after nine in the morning, not as warm as it had been, and she wondered what sort of autumn it would be and when the first snowfall would arrive. Some years it came as early as September but she was having trouble envisioning it, caught in the sense that the summer the town was enduring would not recede easily.

Her eye glimpsed something and she turned her head and took in an unexpected scene. Several people, a few of them in uniform, were scattered on the riverbank.

Cinda stopped, a feeling of dread coming over her.

A hole had been dug; beside it was a body on its back. She somehow knew who it was even before she saw the floppy hat on the ground next to it. She willed herself to walk closer, never taking her eyes off the scene, until she was close enough to see that Wolfpaw had been shot in the forehead, above and between the eyes. The entrance wound was marble-sized with a nearly pristine black ring around it. His eyes were open and Cinda felt his expression seemed peaceful.

Randall was in uniform, standing haplessly off to the side. There were Boulder County officers in uniform but nobody she recognized.

"This is a crime scene, lady," somebody told her. "Don't come any closer."

"Do you know this individual?" said somebody else.

Cinda had stopped moving, looking again at Wolfpaw. "He was my friend," she uttered.

"What was his name?"

Cinda took in a breath. "I never really knew his name."

* * *

It was the middle of the night but Todd wasn't anywhere near falling asleep. Cinda was doing her all-night shift at Boulder County Hospital. She was clearly relieved to have landed a job, grateful she had a friend in Human Resources who'd been willing to vouch for her. Cinda's place, now deathly quiet, was a one-story cabin south of town, just beyond the south fork of the river, no neighbor within a half-mile. The sofa in her den was comfortable enough but Todd's back was killing him.

Cinda had come home from her run stunned and saddened by the loss of her friend. During their conversation at Ossie's, before Todd's attack, she'd told Todd about Wofpaw, how he'd been the one to alert her about the animals' response to Mentex, and that he'd left town in the face of it.

"Why do you think he came back?" asked Todd, as she was getting ready to leave for work.

"I don't know, but I'm certain that coming back is what got him killed. He was trying to help and somebody made him pay for it."

Todd switched on the small table lamp and pulled out his laptop. He turned it on and went to the site where Ossie delivered his "Night Tracks" podcast. The song being broadcast was a gospel infused piece repeating the phrase, "There are strange things happening every day..."

When it ended, Ossie's voice came through. "That was Sister Rosetta Tharpe telling us about the strange things happening in this world... Well, the world's always been strange, back to Cain and Abel, back to Noah putting together that ark. And there are strange things happening in the town of Lynton, Colorado, I'll tell you that for sure."

Todd remained on his back, yet his whole being came to a kind of attention, all but leaning toward the sound of Ossie's voice.

"For one thing, a good friend of mine and a fearless advocate for our community went missing and is still missing. Angie Prez is her name. A lot of you out there must know her. I'm not ready to talk about anybody as vibrant and alive as Angie in the past tense. But I'll tell you, disappearing was not something she did on her own. Somebody's responsible for it and somebody knows where she is.

"There's another friend of mine, Todd Wendt is his name, newly arrived in our community, formerly in the employ of Mentex International, our friends out on Highway 64. The man started asking questions about what the plant managers were up to and the next thing you know, he finds himself charged with a heinous crime that anybody who's come to know him knows he had nothing whatsoever to do with. Not only that, he suffered a brutal attack just outside the Pump-it-Up. You live here and I live here and part of the reason we do is that those things don't happen in Lynton. So I have trouble believing that a couple of thugs just happened to pick the one man in town looking into the internal workings of Mentex. A man who resigned but refuses to go away, which is clearly what they want him to do.

"So what's going on around us? Are the same people responsible for Angie Prez's disappearance also in back of Todd Wendt's very serious predicament? Some other things have gone down that are very peculiar and might somehow be connected. This is a small town, people. If anybody out there knows anything, or suspects anything, it's time to go to the authorities. But you'll need to be cautious because those same authorities are being spoon-fed information that's leading them down a false path.

"I'm gonna shut up for now but I'm not gonna stay quiet. The time for staying quiet is over, my fellow citizens... And now sit back and listen to the immortal Howlin' Wolf who's gonna tell us he's not superstitious, but a black cat just crossed his trail..."

Todd felt as though some kind of wound had been lanced. He closed his eyes and let himself be soothed by the darkness. The pain wasn't over, he knew, but just for the moment it was gone.

PART THREE

DEVASTATIONS

CHAPTER 35

They arrived in cars and trucks and SUVs, until the parking lot was filled. Many had come on foot, crossing the open space beyond Burnham Park. The high school was right at the foot of the mountain, its football and track fields picture perfect. The school had a good reputation, testing well above average in the state. The Lynton Lions, brown and gold, had won the state football championship in 1999, still a source of pride to the community.

Dale Wiggins was moderating this evening's event, a supposedly neutral presence in a three person panel that included Lowell Felker.

"We wanted you all here tonight because of this referendum, which will expand the boundaries of Lynton and this parcel of land will be under the jurisdiction of the township and not Boulder County. For some context and clarification, I'd like to start by introducing a man you've all come to know as he's done so much for Lynton, please welcome, Lowell Felker."

There was scattered applause and Lowell, wearing a buckskin jacket, rose from his seat and took the podium.

"When I first came to this town, seven, eight years ago, I didn't know what to expect. I had Texas in my blood and figured my heart would always be in the Lone Star state. But let me tell you, living here's made me realize there are a whole lot of other stars out there and a lot of them are here, the people of Lynton. What I've come to love about this part of the country, this part of the world, is the sheer physical beauty: the mountains, the rivers, the aspen groves. We all love our aspens out here. Have you ever really thought about how they grow? They don't grow by themselves, like pines or maples. They grow in groups, connected by the same set of roots. And that's how I see the town of Lynton, connected by roots."

And then he spun it, the way he'd been spinning it to Vance these past several months. The way he'd spun it to former mayor Ned Haddock when Lowell first came up with the idea. The way he'd spun it to Dwight Shevney. America needed gas and oil and it couldn't keep being dependent on other countries, most of whom despised America, to get it. But there was plenty of gas in America underground, you just had to drill down to get it. The process unnerved a lot of people. But it wasn't a problem if you could secure the holes with cement casings, and who knew better than the town of Lynton how to make cement, which had long been their only industry?

"It isn't industry against nature – corporations against the environment. It's about natural, God-given prosperity, protected and sustained by *economic* prosperity that puts bread on the tables for the families of our town. Our resources will be preserved but our *industries* will be protected so they can continue to be effective and prosperous... What's going to be different is, we're going to produce like we've been doing, but from now on, for *ourselves*. I hope many of you I've been working with at Mentex will come over to our new facility at a guaranteed higher wage than Mentex has been paying you. You'll be coming with the satisfaction that you're American workers, working for *Americans*, creating a product that'll be, if you'll excuse me, *cementing* the future of our amazing town. We'll be making something that will go out all over the world, and our product will surely make the process of hydraulic fracturing safer and cleaner. Thank you, God bless you, and I look forward to hearing your voices at the ballot box."

Some kept silent, a few were jeering, but those applauding kept it up for a full minute.

Lowell smiled, knowing he'd delivered what he'd come to deliver.

* * *

Had anyone been able to perceive him moving along with the current, they'd have seen three rows of spokes atop a long, thick shell. There were yellow patterns around the eyes, surrounded by star-shaped, fleshy eyelashes. As far as he knew, he was the only one of his kind left here. His two-hundred-fifty pound body had been living in this river for a century and a quarter and its length exceeded two-and-a-half feet. He didn't enjoy swimming; preferred to lie in the mud, tucked beneath the surface, waiting for things to come to him. He flicked his tongue as he surged forward, tempted to draw in a school of smaller fish whose silver forms were flashing in front of him. But, having received the message, he was after something very particular...

* * *

Lonnie had been drinking since late afternoon and now it was nearly dark. The beer they'd stolen from Ossie's was running low; he'd need to organize a mission soon, get hold of another couple of cases.

Trying to make himself feel better by drinking, Lonnie was finding that nothing really helped. He and SB had botched their opportunity with Lowell Felker. Hell, the sonofabitch even refused to pay them anything else for their trouble. And now Lonnie was a killer, except he'd killed somebody he hadn't planned on killing.

It took a few hours to track down the old coot but Lonnie finally found him stretched out in his moldy sleeping bag. SB had chickened out, so Lonnie had to do it all himself. It was pretty cold to put a cap into a guy who was just lying there, but Lonnie had been secretly scared of the dude. Who walks around with a mountain lion at their side like some kind of weird-ass animal trainer? Anybody with that kind of power knew things, and for sure knew too much about Lonnie and SB, so he had to be taken out. Still, it bothered Lonnie. Not that he'd killed him, the dude gave him the creeps, but now Lonnie felt like maybe that old coot had put a curse on him or something.

Standing in the half-light, knee deep in the river, feeling the current wash over his rubber boots as he relieved himself, Lonnie could hear Mental Babs calling out from the bank.

"Get over here, girls, Lonnie's putting on another show."

Meg was up there with them and, as far as he could remember, she'd never been present for his revelation. SB hadn't come around ever since Lonnie told him he'd capped that spooky dude and Lonnie was starting to wonder whether SB was going to go permanently missing.

"Whew, Lonnie," called out Mental Babs. "This must be the longest piss on record."

"The longest everything." Meg giggled.

Lonnie smiled, pleased that somebody new had been initiated into his special feature. He was getting near empty, all the better to make room for more suds. He was pretty wasted but wanted to keep drinking.

Lonnie was shaking it off when a surge of water rose upward, swarming around his torso, followed by a dark, massive blur that thrust viciously toward him. His knees buckled but he remained upright, looking down. The water parted and swirled again, but this time, the rock or whatever it was, went back below the surface. His mind was jumbled. What was happening? Then he was overtaken by a crimson swirl of pain and could hear Babs shrieking from the riverbank.

"What was that – *what the hell was that* – Lonnie, are you all right?"

Remaining upright, he frantically tried to seize his thoughts. He needed to get out of the water, get up on the bank. He pulled his hands toward his waist to tuck his penis back into his jeans. Babs and now Iona and that other girl, what was her name, kept screaming. "Don't move, Lonnie, we're coming down there!"

Lonnie stood, the pain spreading like flame on lighter fluid, blood drenching his thighs and oozing into the rushing water. He kept groping, trying to get hold of that part of him that he'd always felt made him special.

Except, it wasn't there anymore.

* * *

SB parked his 4Runner on the tight street that ran next to the library. From there, it was a short walk into the brush and down the hill to the river. He was going to see the Buddies tonight, or what was left of them, but didn't plan on staying long. Lonnie capping that old guy, especially the way he did it, was pretty much the last straw. SB hadn't had any trouble at all with wasting that guy that Felker wanted them to take out, except they'd botched it. Putting a cap into an old dude who was just lying there asleep; that wasn't right.

So he was heading down to tell Lonnie he was splitting town. Lonnie wouldn't like hearing it, would want to know where SB thought he was going. SB had already decided he'd be vague, telling Lonnie he just needed to chill on a road trip for a couple-few weeks. Truth was, SB had already called his cousin who lived in Long Beach, California and who'd told him, sure come out, crash on the couch till you get yourself settled. SB had never been there but any town that had beach in its name sounded good to him. He just hoped Lonnie wouldn't be able to talk him out of it, or worse, want to come along.

SB was thinking all this when his brain took in that he was hearing voices, female voices. At first he thought they were playing some game but then he heard the terror and alarm and recognized one of them as Mental Babs.

"Oh my God! The blood keeps gushing out of him – oh my God, what are we going to do?"

SB broke into a run. When he reached the clearing, then the riverbank, his eyes probed the dusk. The Draper twins and Meg were standing beside Lonnie, all of them knee deep in water, confused and terrified looks on their faces. Lonnie's hands were clasped below his waist, eyes closed in pain and shock, as though he'd frozen in position and fallen asleep on his feet.

As SB got closer he saw the blood, easing through Lonnie's fingers, completely coating the backs of his hands.

The girls were wide-eyed, gaping. Iona glanced over and spotted SB. "Something attacked Lonnie."

Meg said, "Some... thing came up out of the water and bit him. A crocodile or something."

"It was a turtle," said Mental Babs. "A huge one, it rose up out of the river."

SB didn't say anything, just rushed into the soft current, grabbed hold of Lonnie and hauled him into his arms. Lonnie's lips were trembling but no sound was coming out, just blood oozing from below his waist: blood spreading, blood everywhere.

SB cleared the water but nearly lost his balance ascending the small rise beyond the riverbank, thinking those girls must have been in some kind of shock themselves: *a turtle, a crocodile, the Loch Ness monster for God's sake,* what the hell were they talking about? SB was pretty sure Lonnie had been shot, maybe by some friends of the old coot he'd killed, sniping from the opposite side of the river. "Hang in there, Lon. Hang on, I'm gonna get you taken care of."

But Lonnie was still bleeding like some kind of geyser and was sure to get blood all over SB's freshly cleaned 4Runner. Shit, why hadn't he just left town, why had he dropped by to tell Lonnie goodbye?

* * *

Todd was in Cinda's den when his cell rang and he saw it was her, calling from a hospital phone. It was unusual, as she usually called in the morning, the end of her shift, to see if he wanted her to bring anything from Boulder.

"Everything okay?" he asked.

"A guy was brought in tonight, Lonnie Elkins. A friend of his named Covington carried him in to Emergency. Elkins is pretty short and Covington's a big guy, six and a half feet tall. I mean to say, Elkins *was* short. He died in Covington's back seat on the way here. Loss of blood."

"Is this somebody you knew?"

"Elkins and Covington have been the town bad boys for quite some time. I even busted them once. I don't know why I never put this together before... I think they're the ones who attacked you, Todd. They're exactly the kind of local talent Felker would hire."

Todd thought a moment. "Where's this Covington guy now?"

"Soon as he dropped Elkins, he drove out of here and I'll bet he won't be easy to find."

Todd fell quiet again.

"You still there, Todd?"

"You said Elkins bled to death?"

"Covington at first said it was a gunshot but there was no sign of that. Then he told the admissions nurse that Elkins had been bitten by something down by the river. At first nobody believed it, thinking the guy was trying to cover things up with some story. But the surgeon said Elkins had, in fact, been bitten and that whatever attacked him didn't appear to be human."

CHAPTER 36

Lowell was into his fourth glass of Maker's, kicking back in his den, watching the Dirty Harry festival running all week on Turner Classic Movies. Tonight it was *Sudden Impact*, the one where Harry got to sneer and say, "Go ahead, make my day."

The front doorbell chimed the five note chorus of Home on the Range and Lowell almost called out to Iris to answer it, then remembered she'd gone over to Ossie's to sit in with some bluegrass band, the first time she'd wanted to play since Barry Quinn was bitten by a rattler in the studio. The kid was saying the snake must have crawled into his sound hole while he was rehearsing at Lowell's ranch, that he'd closed up his case there and hadn't opened it until the next morning in the studio. Walking down the long hall, Lowell wondered how long it would take for that lawsuit to be filed.

He crossed the spacious living room that was rarely ever used and opened the door.

Bart Cheever was there, alongside a short, curly-haired guy Lowell didn't recognize. Cheever had never been to the house before and Lowell sensed trouble.

"Come in, fellas. What brings you out here? You wanna come in the den and sit down?"

The two stepped inside but didn't move, clearly not wanting an extended conversation.

"We just need your permission, Lowell," said Cheever. "Something's come up."

"What the hell is it?" Lowell addressed the question, not to Cheever, but to the curly-haired guy. He placed him now. This was Donaldson, the engineer they'd brought on after the spill that night, before Kincaid died. "I'm listening," Lowell told him.

"We have an aquifer issue."

"What the hell is that?"

"It's an underground layer of water-bearing rock."

"Kind of like a huge cavern," said Cheever.

Donaldson glanced at him. "That's not exactly accurate. The point is, the natural gas zone is further down this time. We need to drill through this aquifer to get to it."

Lowell glanced at Cheever. "So go ahead and do it. Why the hell come all the way out here?"

Donaldson shuffled his feet, then looked at Lowell again. "When you drill through an aquifer, there's a greater chance that the cement casing will crack. Hydrocarbons will leak in. If you've got a crack, when you send that fluid down, then back up again, all that will flow into the aquifer. We're talking fracking fluid, methane, mud. You've no control whatsoever as to where it's going to flow underground. You could contaminate an entire water supply. A crack like that has even been known to cause earthquakes."

Lowell's eyes went narrow, like they did when he was thinking hard.

"But you don't *know* that anything will happen?"

"I'm not taking responsibility."

Lowell blew a parcel of air through his cheeks. "Look, Donaldson. I don't know why you need to run out here all lily-livered and ask me about a bunch of stuff I hired you to take care of."

Donaldson shot a glance at Cheever, then turned back to Lowell. "So you're accepting responsibility should the cement down there not hold?"

"You've been hired to drill holes, Donaldson. Just wait while I grab a jacket."

* * *

It feels good to relax, Lowell thought, sitting at his kitchen table. He and Vance and Bart Cheever were sharing a big breakfast.

192

Iris was at the stove, cooking up pancakes to go along with the scrambled eggs and sausage and orange juice and coffee.

Lowell took the red, waxy cap off a fifth of Maker's and poured a shot into everyone's juice glass. "Here's to the end of our testing period. From here on out, we'll be breaking new ground."

"Literally," said Cheever and everybody laughed.

"And here's to tons and tons of cash," said Vance.

"Amen," Lowell added.

Each of them drained his glass.

"I gotta admit," said Lowell, "I was a little concerned about this last baby."

"Who wouldn't be?" said Cheever.

"Well, according to our stalwart engineer, it *was* risky."

"No risk, no reward," said Vance.

"But everything turned out," said Lowell. "We bit through that cave or cavern or whatever the hell Donaldson said was down there. And it didn't seem any different than most of the others."

"And now it's on to our own plant," said Vance.

"What the hell you gonna call it?" asked Cheever.

"The company?" asked Lowell.

"Why don't you name it after little old me?" said Iris, as she stepped over with a platter of steaming pancakes.

"Sounds expensive," said Lowell.

And everybody laughed.

CHAPTER 37

The nest had been formed in late spring, inside a stump on the grounds of the library. As the days grew warmer and longer, the Queen gave the command to move the site to underneath the massive, gray bin. Although such a move was highly unusual and called for a great amount of effort, there was more opportunity for food in this spot. The nest was harder to protect, as there were two-legs coming all through the day and sometimes after dark, dropping what had once held foods and wet things.

All through the summer, the Queen stayed inside the nest, which was expanding every day in size and population. Now, as the days were becoming cooler and shorter, there were over eight hundred workers in the colony, as well as new males and lesser queens, served by the workers.

The Queen sensed her work was nearly over, that her time was ending. Yet one task had to be completed. The two-leg in question had been there before but she had not given the order. This time, a solitary worker let her know that the big red-tailed bird had again come, telling them the prey was on its way and to be ready. The Queen told that worker to spread the message. Hold back but be ready. Once the order was given, this would be an attack like no other. This particular prey was vulnerable to them, much more so than an ordinary two-leg. They would show him no mercy and the Queen's final mission would be completed.

* * *

Even though he worked at Mentex, Vance Dickason was earnest about recycling his personal refuse. Vance, a creature of habit, always made his recycling run on Monday evening, had it written on the Ford Mustang calendar that hung in his kitchen. Once the new company was up and running, the first thing Vance planned to do was buy himself a new Mustang. Tonight he'd agreed to meet Lowell at Ossie's at nine o'clock. Iris was scheduled to do a set and Lowell liked Vance to be around as much as possible when Lowell and Iris were out in public. Hell, Vance had even been asked a few times whether he and Iris had a thing going.

The recycling bins were the only ones of their kind in Lynton. There were three, set on a raised wooden platform, each the size of a fishing boat, painted gun metal gray. One was for paper, one for cardboard, the other for glass and plastic. Vance often ran into someone he knew during these excursions, and once he'd encountered a stringer from the Boulder Observer who'd interviewed him. When his picture appeared in the paper with the caption: *Vance Dickason of Mentex Takes Recycling Seriously* it had won big points with the boss.

Vance was in a cheery mood, which had not been his usual state lately. Since Angie Prez's death, he'd been fighting off cloudy feelings. They weren't remorseful, more like a vague dread that somehow he and Lowell would be found out.

Vance held a plastic bin under each arm. He hadn't eaten at home much that week so there were only a half-dozen glass bottles, along with assorted plastic, filling about two-thirds of one container. The other was half-full, newspaper and junk mail mostly, along with a few bills. He deposited the paper, shoving the container top-end-first into the space and letting the papers drop to the top of the pile. When he stepped toward the other bin, all the metal doors were closed, so he slid open the nearest one. He vigorously hurled the contents onto the massive pile of cans and bottles. You weren't supposed to break anything but Vance tended to ignore that, especially at moments like this, when no one was around. Ever since he'd been a kid he'd enjoyed the sound of glass shattering.

Standing there in his black jeans and black t-shirt, Vance felt an odd sensation on his lower left leg. He lifted it to scratch his calf and became aware of not just his leg but a sharp, harsh sensation around his waist, beneath his shirt. Vaguely aware of a growing hum, he flailed his arms frantically, realizing he was under attack, a swarm so thick it was like he had been somehow dropped into a swirling funnel. His neck was encircled and his ears were being assaulted with a furious buzzing, his mouth and his nose and eyes, every inch of skin, covered by a swarm.

Vance rushed to the edge of the platform between the recycling bins. His feet became entangled and his body tumbled down the small set of wooden steps to the concrete. He shot back up, carrying the swarm with him. He felt if he could reach his car, he might somehow escape.

As he ran into the street a Hyundai Sonata, carrying a couple in their seventies, braked at the sight of the whirling body completely engulfed in a tornado of black and yellow, rolling frantically across the width of the street, kicking and flailing.

Inside the car, the woman said to her husband, "Should we get out? Do we need to do something?"

The man sat immobile, taking in the horrific sight.

Then, as though some signal had been given, the swarm swept away from the body that was now scarcely moving.

Vance was folded inward, his stomach cramping viciously, heart rushing as a result of tachycardia and constricting capillaries.

The driver got out of his car and walked timidly toward the victim.

The face and arms were hideously swollen and distorted. The body underwent one final seizure, then lay lifeless.

* * *

Lowell had been drinking ever since getting the news about Vance. Pacing, he crossed the front room, his eye caught by a pair of headlights from the driveway. Who the hell would be here at this hour?

Lowell went to the door, thought better about opening it and instead opened the drawer in the foyer where he kept his .44 Magnum, its considerable heft reassuring as he pulled the front door toward him. Two people were approaching, a man and a woman. Lowell stepped out onto the porch.

"Who's there – what do you want?"

The two stopped walking, clearly having seen the pistol glistening under the porch light.

"It's Todd Wendt, Lowell. We need to talk."

Slurring, Lowell said, "I thought you'd be locked up by now."

"And it's me, Cinda Rigg."

"The former rent-a-cop. Are you two an item?" He chuckled. "I'd say you were made for each other."

Todd stepped forward. "What happened to Vance, Lowell… if it can be stopped, you're the one who can put a stop to it."

"Things were going fine until you showed up around here. All that's been happening, maybe it's you who's the cause of it. Maybe you're cursed, or something."

Todd was almost to the porch, Cinda a step behind him. "You know that's not true, Lowell. And we both know you're at risk yourself."

Lowell raised the pistol and cocked it, leveling it at Todd's chest. "Get the hell off my ranch."

Todd exhaled, realizing he'd been holding his breath. He turned to Cinda. "Let's leave him to himself. Whatever's going to happen is going to happen."

Lowell kept the gun pointed at Todd and Cinda as they climbed into the Cherokee and backed out of the driveway.

CHAPTER 38

It was mid-morning at The Wagging Tail and Todd was sipping coffee, reading the front page article in the Lynton Record. The exciting news, and it was characterized as such, was that a new cement plant would be opening, owned and overseen by Lowell Felker. While it would be supplying cement to companies all over the globe that were engaged in fracking, there would be no fracking in the town itself after an initial set of tests.

Todd looked up and saw that he had company. Lieutenant Nieman of the Boulder County Police was standing at his table.

"Coffee's pretty good here, isn't it, Wendt?"

Todd didn't ask him to sit down but Nieman pulled up a chair anyway. Glancing over, Todd saw Nieman's sidekick in line at the register. "You're not going to invite your partner to join us?"

"We're getting stuff to go. We just came out here to put the finishing touches on the arrest we've made in the Angie Prez case."

Todd felt his system jolt a few knots. "You found Angie?"

"Naw, but we've got a very strong suspect. Seems Angie was investigating the accidental death of a Mentex employee and found out the poor bastard's brother's been screwing the wife. They were trying to squeeze Mentex for money while trying to keep their little love affair a secret. Angie was going to spoil all that, so this creep, Kent Kincaid's his name, started making threats. Our cells are packed, so we've got him locked up in a very tiny cell in Lynton's very tiny jail."

"How do you know he's the right man?" asked Todd.

"Angie Prez's neighbor, who just returned from a trip to Europe, positively ID'd him as confronting Prez at her apartment."

Todd took it in, but something told him he was hearing a scenario tied up in too neat a box.

Nieman pushed back his chair. "And there's more good news for you, Wendt. The Sorrento case is still open, but it seems your accuser stole a set of credit cards from one of the houses she was cleaning and has been using them all over Nevada. If they catch her out there, and it's only a matter of time, we might not even be able to get her back here to testify."

* * *

Fifty, Dale Wiggins thought to himself; *how in the world did I get to be fifty?* He was driving along one of the back roads, enjoying how the fields spread out all around him; driving east, so the road in front was flat, the mountains in his rear view mirror. It seemed like not that long ago he was attending CU, smoking pot, drifting through his classes, falling in love with this part of the world after leaving Missouri behind. He thought he'd seen mountains before coming out here as every summer of his childhood, his parents would take him and his brother and two sisters to the Ozarks. But once he arrived in Colorado and saw the Rockies, he knew that these were the mountains for him.

And now he was going to go up higher even than any mountain. Should he smoke some crank beforehand? Naw, the natural high would be enough. *Fifty freaking years old* and to mark the occasion, Dale Wiggins was going to jump out of an airplane.

The whole thing was a gift from his buddy, Terry Anderwater, who was in charge of Valmont's tiny airport. For years, driving near there, Dale had seen evidence of all kinds of aerial activity, skydivers, para-gliders, hot air balloons. On a clear, warm day like this, he'd scan the sky to see what was floating. Well, today it would be him.

Terry had called that morning to see if Dale was still game.

"Hell yes, I'm down for it."

"Great, man, I packed the chute already. We'll take off soon as you get here."

Was Dale afraid? No, he told himself, just a little amped at the prospect of doing something he'd always been curious about. Fifty, *freaking fifty*. Not only was there no time like the present, there was no time *but* the present.

Fifty seemed to be a good point to take stock of your life. What you'd done and what you'd left undone. Dale had never married, had no kids. Didn't have much money in the bank, but that would change soon. In a culture that valued accomplishment and the accumulation of wealth, Dale was going to end up rich. He owned a very small percentage of Felker's new cement venture, but a small percentage of a fortune can still be a fortune. Of course, Shevney had all but held a gun to his head but Dale was at peace with things now. One aspect of the referendum's outcome had surprised Dale. Then he freshly realized that when it came down to it, people were inclined and willing and eager to vote their pocketbooks. He and Felker didn't even need to rig the outcome; the people of Lynton voted to make way for the cement that would be used for fracking all over the world.

* * *

"You ready, Wiggs?" Terry called out from the pilot's seat.

Dale, poised at the open doorway, gave him thumbs up. Terry had circled the target once, just so Dale could take it all in, and now he was going for real. Standing in a half-crouch, Dale remembered a line someone once said about parachuting: *why would anybody want to jump out of a perfectly good airplane?*

Dale Wiggins, fifty years old, cycler, stoner, ex-coke dealer, accessory to a decades old homicide and mayor of Lynton, Colorado, took a deep breath. The instant he stepped out, there'd be nothing to hold onto, nothing holding him up, the law of gravity his master, except, of course, once the ripcord opened, as Terry assured him it would. "Now, Wiggs, go now."

Dale tipped forward and then was out, free falling through a vast and empty space, wind whipping around him like waves in an endless body of water. "If that chute doesn't open," Terry had instructed, "you've got your emergency cord, so yank that. But trust me, Wiggs, this will be amazing, and I'd never put you in a spot you couldn't get out of."

Dale was falling, the ground getting closer, like it was erupting or being shoved up at him... that goddamn chute better open. He felt a whoosh above him; his body jerked and his legs splayed forward, then his shoulders, torso, hips... everything settled and he was floating, the ground which had appeared harsh and chaotic only a few seconds before spread out soft and welcoming.

Man, this was sweet, next time he'd pull his own cord, maybe be high all the way through it. Above and to his left, Terry's Cessna was banking right, preparing to return to the airport. Maybe he could get Terry to share a joint with him in celebration, the guy stopped stoning years before but maybe Dale could goad him into it.

Then his eyes went to something else, a huge bird, an eagle or a hawk, twenty, maybe thirty yards away, flapping its huge wings like it was treading air. Dale felt himself smile. *The things you see up here.* Then... *What was that?*

He craned his neck back from the harness and saw a mass of black swarming directly above him. *What the hell?* A flock of crows, each of them identically black like it was all the same bird, except that there were scores of them, a hundred or more, flapping and squawking and swooping and circling and *oh my God* a few of them, no, several of them, *lots* of them were clinging to the nylon suspension lines attached to the domed canopy. *What the hell is this, what's going on?*

Dale's mind was flipping like a fish on a slippery deck. The crows were frantically pecking and gnawing, scratching and clawing, tearing at the cords that supported the only thing keeping Dale Wiggins from dropping to the earth. Dale's heart thudded and his breath went cold as one, then another of the nylon cords frayed, disengaging as a result of being ferociously attacked. His protective nylon halo appeared to burst, then jerk away as though yanked by an unseen hand. Dale Wiggins, fifty years old, cycler, stoner, ex-coke dealer, accessory to a decades-old homicide and mayor of Lynton, Colorado, dropped to the earth with ever increasing speed as the flock of crows cawed and cackled and flapped triumphantly toward the mountains.

CHAPTER 39

Todd took a walk by himself while Cinda was gone to Valmont doing errands. He felt that whatever danger he was in had passed, at least for now. Cinda lived just south of his place so it was easy for him to get back on his old bird watching route further along Peach Orchard Road, to the unnamed and unpaved road that had the river on one side, the occasional farmhouse on the other.

After about ten minutes, even the farmhouses weren't present, only a mountain face on his left, with the river and open space on his right. This was where it was most tranquil, where he could not only spot the birds, but could hear their calls and songs. Except something was coming clear to him, walking that back road.

The birds, varied and profuse during his previous walks, simply weren't there anymore.

Todd stopped walking and listened. No bird trills, no buzzing insects, nothing. Just the wind, as well as what one so rarely experienced...

Total silence.

A wave of fear rose on the back of his neck, the first time since the attack that he'd felt much besides the severe pain to his lower back. Now, his back enduring a dull ache that did not interfere with his mobility, he swiftly made his way back to Cinda's place.

She was in the kitchen, taking groceries out of their bags.

"I thought you weren't going to go out unless I was with you," she said.

"I was just going a bit stir crazy."

Cinda stepped over and took hold of his hand. "Since you were able to take a walk, you must be well on your way to recovery."

Todd laughed. "Well, I feel better, that's for sure."

Cinda took another step forward and gave him what was

much more than a friendly kiss. Todd was surprised but was right there with it. When they came up from it, she took hold of his hand and said, "I think it's time to see just how good you *do* feel."

They didn't undress each other but undressed themselves, flinging clothes in every direction, then all but dove onto the bed, where there were no words, just breath and touch and embrace. Both feverishly ready in no time, Cinda took hold of Todd and guided him to her and they moved, gently at first, then picked up speed and Cinda was crying out and Todd heard a deep tone rising from his gut to his chest and up through his neck, making his breath even more heated and resonant. And then there was a vibration, like a nudging at first, then a shove like some outside force had entered the room causing everything to rattle and shake. As this wave kept growing in intensity and strength, Todd uttered, "What's going on, Cinda?"

She pulled back from him, rolling to the side of the bed as the motion intensified, sending her onto the floor. "I don't know!" she cried.

Every object in the room was jiggling and rattling, vertically, horizontally, every which way. Todd felt disoriented, the sensations peculiar and extreme, yet somehow familiar from his years in California and Mexico City. "Earthquake," he said. "It's an earthquake."

He left the bed and, everything shaking about them, helped Cinda up from the floor. "C'mon," he said and led them to the open doorway.

It had only been seconds but felt like an eternity as the shaking intensified.

"How long is it going to last?" asked Cinda.

Todd pulled her to him and the wave seemed to reach a peak, having splintered or shattered or disturbed everything in its wake. As suddenly as it started, it was as if a gigantic hand had said, "Enough."

Stillness and quiet as Todd and Cinda held each other tight in the doorway.

"Well," Todd said, "I felt the earth move, how about you?"

* * *

Aftershocks continued throughout the day and into the evening. None was as large as the five-point-five quake, but still they were frequent and unsettling. According to the local news, there was no loss of life but significant property damage, especially to older structures.

Cinda wasn't scheduled to work that night, and this time, when she and Todd went to bed, there was no other force but their own delight and discovery of each other.

The following morning, Todd and Cinda got together a picnic basket: turkey and cheese sandwiches, salad with tomato and red peppers, some leftover blueberry pie, water and juice. They tossed it into the back of Cinda's roughed-up but reliable Jeep Cherokee.

Driving east for a few miles toward Boulder, Cinda took a right onto Middle Peak Highway, which was a highway only for a few miles, then turned into a narrow, winding, two lane road, only a low metal guardrail as a barrier against a drastic drop off.

As they wove ever higher, the guard rail was gone and the road became gravel and then dirt as though sending a message to those winding upwards that they were increasingly on their own.

"Pretty challenging driving," said Todd, knowing immediately it was a needless comment.

"Sure is," said Cinda, as they rounded a curve. "If you go off the road in Lynton, you go into a ditch. Up here, you go off a cliff."

They passed a firehouse with two trucks parked beside a small building, one truck, old and faded yellow; one big and red and gleaming. Todd thought how flimsy and useless either vehicle would seem against a raging wildfire. The houses, once fairly in evidence, were now remote.

They reached a waterfall and Todd said, "Looks like a good spot. Should we pull over?"

"Let's go a little higher," said Cinda. "I have a place in mind, just above Rabbit's Foot Rock."

"What's Rabbit's Foot Rock?"

"You'll see."

A few minutes later, they were at a huge body of water contained by a massive cement barrier.

"My God," uttered Todd. "That's an incredible dam."

"It holds back tons of water that would otherwise be flowing through every part of Lynton."

"Wait a sec, pull over right here."

Cinda eased the Cherokee off to the side and Todd opened the door and stepped out. Just crossing the road he could tell how much thinner the air was at this elevation. He had his binoculars with him and trained them on the wall of the reservoir.

"What is it," asked Cinda. "You're seeing something?"

Todd looked a minute more, then handed the binoculars to Cinda.

Peering into them, she chuckled. "Beavers there, bobbing on the surface."

"They look like baby seals or something. How big do those things get?"

"They can tip fifty pounds. A yard long as well. They have it pretty good up here."

"Over there, is one of them flapping its tail? Looks like a canoe paddle."

"Any one of those can chew through a whole tree trunk in less than an hour. They don't call them busy beavers for nothing."

"Must be twelve, fifteen of them there on the surface."

"There's likely a lot more underwater. They can hold their

breath for fifteen minutes. I've seen them, but not this many at once. The buggers must be building something. C'mon, I'm hungry, aren't you?"

Todd smiled, looking one last time at the reservoir. "You know what's so great about this, those beavers working the way they are?"

Cinda shook her head.

"They're doing what they're made to do. It's all so... ordinary."

CHAPTER 40

Lowell woke up, as was the usual case of late, with a fierce hangover. He threw on some clothes and walked to the kitchen, just down the hall. Spooning coffee into its filter, he heard a sound coming from the garage. Did he park the Escalade in there last night, or had he left it out in the driveway? That's right, he'd definitely parked in the garage because he'd argued with Iris about it before she'd gone off to bed. The garage door was wide open when he'd come home and she'd claimed she hadn't left it like that. The argument escalated and she stormed off to her hole-in-the-wall apartment.

Lowell crossed the kitchen and opened the door that led into the garage. He must have been in a hurry to get in the house last night, the driver's side door of the Escalade was half-open. He stepped off the landing and into the gray daylight seeping in from outside.

On his way to shut the door of the SUV, he heard that sound again, coming from outside. Lowell felt a wave of apprehension. What was out there? Then he was overcome with a feeling that it was daylight, he was at home, there was nothing he was going to let spook him.

Lowell stepped over to the button that activated the garage door. There were actually two doors that operated separately but only half of the garage housed a vehicle, in this case, the Escalade. The other side was littered with a dozen cardboard boxes he was storing for Iris. She kept promising she'd go through them, at least cut their number in half, but so far had not made a move in that direction. Sometimes he wondered what the hell she did all day.

The door was making that grating, rumbling sound and was halfway up, the outside scene steadily being revealed. Something caught Lowell's eye, a black mass on the other side of the gradually ascending wooden door. More and more was revealed until Lowell could only stand there, frozen, blinking dumbly in response. The space was fully open and Lowell could take in the entire image.

A quarter-ton bear, risen to its hind legs, its gleaming eyes trained on him. Lowell lunged back to send the door downward. Before he could reach the button, the bear was on all fours, bounding toward him with breathtaking speed. Lowell pressed the button and the door once again descended but was too slow. The bear entered the garage an inch below the descending door as it closed behind him.

Lowell was standing in his garage, tools neatly arranged on the walls, Iris's boxes strewn, the Escalade, silent and shiny. The only thing wrong with the picture and undercutting the mundane nature of it, was the enormous creature leering at him, snorting like a boxer awaiting the opening bell.

Knowing he would have to fight, Lowell could all but see the steam gusting from the beast's nose and mouth. It appeared demonic as it lunged at him with stunning agility. Lowell was caught flatfooted, the bear butting his chest with its massive head, sending him crashing into the wall, smashing the back of his head against the harsh wood.

And now Lowell was flat on the cement floor, legs splayed out in front of him as the bear raked his cheek with its claws. He felt the bear's powerful jaws clamp onto his shoulder, its teeth sinking in. He swung his right fist and caught the bear on the side of the skull and surprisingly, the animal released its hold, pulling back its head and looking at Lowell with what seemed to be a stunned expression.

Lowell saw his moment and rolled to the right, but the bear recovered and pounced on him. As Lowell tried to roll out from underneath, there was simply too much weight, too much power. He felt the hot breath on his neck, could hear the beast snorting and blowing as it again gnawed his shoulder. Lowell's terror gave way to rage and he rolled to his left just as the bear was rearing up, a hunk of his flesh between its jaws. Lowell sprang to his feet and the bear looked up at him, again projecting some primitive version of surprise.

Lowell glanced at the wall and saw a wrench, a hammer, a power drill. He lunged for the drill and activated it just as the bear was on him again. Lowell shoved the long silver nose of the drill into the bear's left eye. Blood spun and swirled and Lowell saw he might be able to get to the only sanctuary available. He leaped toward the half-open door of the Escalade and slammed it behind him.

Outside, the bear, bloody and half-blinded, was growling ferociously and slapping the air in front of him with bloody paws. Sprawled across the front seat, Lowell saw that, in the previous night's debacle, he'd left the keys in the ignition. He gave a twist and the dashboard lit up. Lowell pressed the lock button and the locks clicked downward.

The beast was furious, roaring, on its hind legs, clawing at the Plexiglas window as Lowell looked at him through the glass. "Fuck you!" Lowell screamed. "Fuck you, you fucking monster!"

He pressed the plastic rectangular button and the garage door behind him rumbled upwards. To Lowell's dismay and delight, the bear seemed to shrug its huge shoulders and he saw it lope away from the driver's side window. He picked up its massive form in the rear view mirror, his delight spreading as the bear, seemingly resigned, moved out of the garage and down the driveway, away from the house.

Lowell took a deep breath. He'd drive himself to the hospital. His shoulder hurt like hell but there was plenty of flesh there to sew up. As he turned over the engine, his eyes caught a fresh image in the rear view mirror.

A black bear, a second one, was slowly rising up in the back seat.

* * *

Dwight Shevney was angry. Bart Cheever had called and told him about Lowell Felker getting mauled and eaten in his own garage. His mistress had found him, said Cheever, then got in her car and drove to her parent's home in Durango. What was the world coming to? Not only that, but Felker's assistant, that kid who had driven him up here, had been killed in some bizarre way, stung to death or something. The mayor of Lynton had bounced while skydiving and witnesses claimed it was a flock of birds who'd attacked his chute. Shevney told Cheever that if anybody else met a weird death, Cheever included, he didn't want to hear about it.

Secretly he was scared, had even got on his knees and prayed. Shevney believed in the End of Days. He and Ron Reagan, rest his soul, had even discussed it once in the East Room of the White House. God could be hard and judgments could be harsh. Why else would He allow so many terrible things to happen? Mauled to death and eaten, that was the fate of Lowell Felker. He wasn't a good man, Shevney knew; Felker was a fornicator and a drinker. Men like him were always looking for the big score that would set them up for life. Shevney knew the big scores were already settled and the Lowell Felkers of the world would forever have their noses pressed to the glass.

Still, the man's death scared him. What was going on to bring about all this sudden carnage? Dwight Shevney found himself hiding indoors ever since getting the news. But today he felt too big, too powerful to hide out like a rabbit. This dawn, he'd put on his gear and loaded his rifle and set out for the woods, not telling Marcel or anybody else his intentions.

There was a chill in the air but he couldn't see his breath.

He trod carefully. He didn't know what he was after but he wanted to bag something. It was his species who were the enlightened ones; he was no beast, what brutality he inflicted was necessary and just and purposeful.

Almost to the woods now, he saw movement and then a manifestation which astounded him. *A buffalo, how did it get here?* He'd stocked the woods with deer and elk and antelope, but this was astounding. Almost reverently, he raised his rifle and sighted. The massive animal gazed at him, untroubled and somehow at peace. Shevney sighted right above the dumb tranquil eyes, in the middle of the forehead.

About to squeeze the trigger, Shevney became aware of movement to the right of where he was sighting. He swung the rifle subtly in that direction, astonished to see an elk with an expansive rack, pressing forward from the thick growth. Muscled and massive, the animal looked to be approaching half a ton, the most spectacular of its species he'd ever laid eyes upon. Shevney swung his weapon slightly left and saw the buffalo still frozen in his sight, as if asking whether he or the huge elk would be the target.

Utterly distracted, Shevney had no awareness that something was charging, a beige streak, soundlessly behind him. Bounding then leaping, the lion's front legs slammed into the middle of Shevney's back, who lurched forward, the gun flipping up and toward him, left hand on the stock and right finger on the trigger. The explosion sent the missile into Shevney's forehead, exiting upwards, taking with it the top of his skull.

Then silence again as the lion, with but a brief a glance behind, bounded past the soundless tableau of the buffalo and elk before fading into the dense woods.

CHAPTER 41

Shevney's death made national news. A hunting accident, which neither Todd nor Cinda connected with the Mentex related deaths. In Lynton, Lowell Felker's hideous end was on everyone's lips. "Do you think it's over?" Cinda asked while she and Todd were having dinner in her kitchen.

"I hope to God," uttered Todd although consumed with a dread he couldn't shake. Something in the air, in his gut, told him it wasn't over. Plus, it had been pouring non-stop for seventy-two hours. His cell rang and it was Ossie.

"What you up to, Todd?"

"Just, you know, absorbed with the events of the day."

"I want you to come over to the bar and celebrate." For the first time since the night Todd met him, Ossie seemed to have been sampling his own goods.

"It's pouring out there. Can we take an actual rain check?"

"A man gets awarded the Best Ale in America by the New York Times and nobody will even drink with him?"

"Ossie, that's fantastic."

Ossie laughed. "I know it's storming out there. I just needed to tell you. The phone's been ringing non-stop and I want to talk with you about handling PR for Ossie's Ebony. We're going national, baby. Let's sit down, soon as we can."

* * *

In the dream, Todd was locked in a cell. The walls and floor were smooth cement. One thin crack ran along the wall facing him, culminating in a wider crack where the base of the wall met the floor. He held a rusty and crumpled spoon and with that he dug into the lower crack, knowing eventually the entire crack in the wall would grow wider and give way.

He awoke in the dark in Cinda's bed, with her beside him. It was still coming down outside. He thought again about how close Cinda's house was to the river but felt that even with all this rain it would not be enough to overflow its banks. Yet something about the dream was spreading inside of him and it was anything but comforting.

Cinda stirred beside him. "You're awake?"

"Go back to sleep, I'm just a little restless."

"It hasn't stopped raining."

"No, it hasn't."

"I'm starting to get worried," she said, sitting up.

"You know how things come to you in the middle of the night, things you haven't consciously thought of?"

Cinda reached over and switched on the bedside lamp.

Adjusting to the light, Todd continued. "What about the birds all leaving town, going up into the mountains. Probably other creatures as well. I think they knew an earthquake was coming, and maybe they know something else is coming, and that's why they haven't come back."

Cinda sat up a little higher.

"Those beavers we saw," said Todd. "How strange that there were so many of them, diving underneath the surface, then coming up for air, then diving down again. I know you said they were building something, but what if they weren't?"

"Weren't what?"

"Weren't *building*. What if they were *taking something away?* After that earthquake and those aftershocks, what if Rabbit's Foot Rock got a crack in the dam? And what if those beavers have just been helping it along?" Todd felt fully awake, consumed with dread. "With something like a flood, who sounds the town alarm?"

"The precinct. That's where all the emergency tests are run from."

Todd scooted to the edge of the bed. "We need to get over there and convince somebody to sound the alarm. Then somebody needs to go up to Rabbit's Foot Rock and see if there's a crack in the dam."

"What if we're wrong?" asked Cinda.

"If we're wrong, we'll be waking a lot of people up. If we're right we'll be saving a lot of lives."

* * *

Ginger was beside herself. Everything that could have gone wrong, had. Of course she hadn't wanted or expected Frank to die, but at least he left not knowing that she and Kent were planning a life together. But Kent had shadowed Angie Prez and she turned up missing and the cops wanted to make it easy on themselves by blaming Kent. She just wished Kent hadn't spilled when the cops were questioning him that he and Ginger were in love and that was why he wanted Prez to back off.

Nobody had taken it very well. Frank and Kent's sister, who'd always favored Frank and despised Kent, insisted on taking the kids for a while and Ginger hadn't put up much of a fight. She wasn't really functioning. Money was tight but she couldn't imagine what kind of shitty job she'd need to find, so she was avoiding the whole thing, biting her nails, eating junk and fretting over Kent.

It didn't help that he was locked up in town, just a few blocks away, on the other side of the river. In their phone conversations, he told her that most nights it was just him and this punk deputy, nobody he could even talk to. But since he'd told her that Ginger couldn't stop thinking, why not just go on over there and bust him out and start driving? West probably, maybe to Vegas, even though she'd never been there or Reno, where she'd never been either but which seemed less obvious and easier to hide in. She'd miss the kids but their lives were poisoned anyway because the arrest made not only the Record but the Boulder Observer, and everybody knew about it now. The few times Ginger had left the house, at the post office and the bank and the grocery store, people looked at her like she was walking around naked. Kids were teasing April and Kara, and Ginger could only hope that when they were older and found out what love was all about, true love, not some sort of habit or obligation, they'd cut their mom a little slack and not think she was a monster.

The rain, goddammit, when was it going to stop? She couldn't stand the thought of her man locked up in a cold, damp cell, only because he loved her. Ginger went to the closet. There was a footstool shoved back in there and she pulled it to her. She got on the stool and reached up, feeling the muscles strain in the small of her back, God she'd been tense lately. She groped around, and there it was in its leather holster. Ginger pulled it to her, then stepped off the footstool.

She knew how to use it, Frank had made sure of that. She'd protested at first when he took her to the firing range in Valmont but he convinced her, saying, 'What if I'm not home and somebody breaks in the house?'

Ginger ended up enjoying those times. Frank was reluctant to admit it, but it got to the point where she was a better shot than he was. She liked this piece, a .22 that fit nicely in her hand and there wasn't much kick to it. Could she really use it if she had to? Damn right, she could, what more was there to lose? Without even thinking, she pulled a suitcase out of the closet, opened it on the bed and started tossing things inside, the things she and Kent would need once they got to Reno or wherever the hell they ended up.

* * *

At the precinct, Randall could hear the rain thrashing and rattling on the roof and wondered how long it could take an assault like this. The roof had been damaged during a freak hailstorm earlier in the summer and nobody had got around to getting it fixed. It was leaking, he could hear it in the corner of the tight room that served as a kitchen. He hoped it didn't start leaking inside the cell where Kent Kincaid was locked up.

The jail was older, much older than the room where Randall had his desk. The precinct room was an open, cement-bordered space that had been added on in the sixties or seventies. The jail itself was ancient and spooky. Legend was that some drunk who'd carved up a prostitute back in the 1880s hung himself in the very cell that was now occupied by Kent Kincaid, and not only the drunken spirit but that of the dead woman were said to haunt the structure that had been standing back then.

Randall didn't like working alone. That was a condition less likely to happen when Cinda Rigg had been on the force, but now he was by himself at least every other night. He'd done what he'd been paid to do, pull Cinda over on South Center and go straight for the driver's seat to confiscate the bottle that was planted.

"Hey, man, would you come in here a minute?"

That was Kincaid shouting. Randall didn't like the guy but it was unusual for him to be raising his voice. Usually, he just sat and stared at the wall.

Randall trudged down the short hallway. Kincaid was off his bunk, fingers wrapped around the iron bars. Randall could see what the matter was even before Kincaid told him. Dammit, there was water, and not just a trickle but a steady flow from the ceiling, coming right down on top of the toilet.

"What are you gonna do about that?" asked Kincaid.

Randall glanced over. The water, spreading over the closed toilet seat, was flowing onto the stone floor.

"I'm gonna hope it stops raining," said Randall.

"C'mon, man. It ain't stopped for three days. Sounds like it ain't about to stop. You can't expect me to sit here while everything around me gets soaked."

Randall turned away. "This is a jail, mister. Not the Brown Palace Hotel."

Randall smirked as he walked down the hall. The line wasn't original but he'd delivered it well. Still, he was concerned. That was a small space and it wouldn't take long for the water to rise. That rain, why the hell wouldn't it quit? Hell, they were a stone's throw from the river. What if the banks overflowed and the jail got flooded? There was no basement, nowhere to confine a suspected murderer. He'd have to keep his gun on Kincaid while he cuffed him. That was a part of his training that Randall had never been good at. For somebody accused of murder, Kincaid didn't seem especially dangerous. But Randall was alone in this. He'd need to call for back-up even though they were, since Cinda, shorthanded. With all this swarming in his head, Randall decided to step outside and take a look at the river.

He grabbed a flashlight and one of the rain slickers in the supply closet. Turning on the light, he stepped out. There were rivulets of water right outside the front door, just a couple of inches but clearly spreading and rising. The jail structure was causing the water to eddy out in opposite directions toward the street. There was nothing blocking the water from the river and what if it was breaching?

His question was answered almost immediately. A tide of water was pushing up and out from the banks, flowing straight at him. For reasons he didn't know, Randall kept moving forward as though by doing so he could somehow push back the flow. Then he stopped. The water was calf-deep and coming at him and if he kept heading into it, it would be knee deep. The force was strong; it was all he could do to keep his balance.

Randall stood there, rain pounding, river water rushing around him. He glanced at the jail. A dim light peeked out from inside. The prisoner was in there. Should Randall get him out? But he was an accused murderer. Randall wasn't convinced he could deal with him and a gun and handcuffs and rising water.

He could hold the gun on him and demand that the prisoner put the cuffs on himself but who knew if he would cooperate?

Yes, Randall needed back-up, some support. The water was nearly up to his knees. The jail had a stone foundation but was surely going to take water. How long did he have, ten minutes, fifteen?

Garrison was the deputy-on-call. He lived a minute or two away, just on the other side of the bridge. Randall didn't want to go back in there and mess with a phone call. He needed help now.

The County SUV was high enough to push through the rising water. Randall hopped in, turned on the engine and backed out. Garrison had to be home, who'd be out on a night like this? He'd get him to come back and lend a hand while the two of them collected the prisoner and drove him... where? Probably the Boulder County Justice Center, where the sonofabitch should have been taken in the first place.

* * *

Kent was standing on his cot in the dimly-lit cell. "Hey, hey, man. Officer. Where the hell are you? What the hell's going on here?"

The cop had gone outside, Kent heard the door close and didn't hear him come back in. All he could hear were weird sounds from outside. He needed to get out of this cell. Water had been seeping in for some time. Now it was swirling, rushing, and the sound that came with it was spooky as hell. Then what little light there was went out.

No, this was wrong. No light, and water rushing through the hall and into the cell. Total blackness, like he was trapped in a mineshaft. "I need help," he called out, strong at first, then trembling and weak.

Kent couldn't help it, his lips kept moving. At first there was no sound but then sound came bubbling out of him, like a petrified child. "Dear Lord, come get me out of this. I've done some bad things, but I never killed anyone. Not like they said. I done some things I'm ashamed of. I wish Ginger hadn't been Frank's wife. Yeah, that was wrong. That shouldn't have happened but, Lord, I'm sorry. Get me out and I'll make it as right as I can. Frank, I'm sorry. When I see you, I'll... apologize and make it up to you. I hope I get to see you, Frank. I know you're in heaven. You were a good brother, Frank, and I wasn't, but I hope I get to see you..."

* * *

Todd and Cinda had to abandon the Cherokee a block from the precinct. Now they were walking toward the one-story structure, each clutching a flashlight, not a word passing between them as they trudged through the thigh-deep water.

The door was unlocked and the precinct was pitched in darkness.

"The power's off," said Cinda. "But the alert system's linked to the county's main generator, so it should work."

"Hey, who's out there?" A voice from one of the cells.

Todd stepped over to the small hallway while Cinda made her way to the back room. He shone his flashlight into the first cell.

"Get me out," the voice said. "I'm gonna die in here."

"Why's there nobody on duty?" asked Todd.

"I don't know, man. But you've got to get me the hell out. This place is taking in water."

Todd felt his whole body flinch in response to the deafening siren that Cinda activated. A recorded voice accompanied the din. "This is an alert from Lynton Township Disaster Center. This is not a test. You are to leave your homes immediately and make your way to higher ground. Repeat, this is not a test!"

Todd squinted in response to Cinda's flashlight trained on

his face.

"We've got to go, Todd. No time to lose."

"This guy's locked up in here and nobody's around. We can't leave him."

There was a moment, then Cinda said. "I'll get the keys, but then we, all of us, need to get out of here."

* * *

The windshield wipers were useless. Heading along Third, Ginger was pretty sure she had only one headlight. She'd always despised this piece-of-shit Blazer. She didn't want to stop and check out the headlight and get herself soaked. She and Kent would need to get it fixed first chance they got and hope it didn't get them pulled over in the meantime.

The closer she got to North Center Street, the more water was swirling in front of her. She hoped she didn't get the brakes wet, that was all she needed. So much water, it looked like it was gushing up out of the gutters. She turned down Edgewood Lane, which bordered the river on this side of town. That's when she heard the warning siren for the second time in a couple of minutes. She'd heard them for years but this was the first time they'd said it wasn't a test. Could that be right? No matter, there was no turning back now.

The bridge was an old cement structure that could accommodate one vehicle at a time. Ginger eased forward. The front tires rolled onto the bridge. The tread on them was dismal; Ginger hoped they would take, not sway, on the soaked surface. Then she heard something, a cracking sound, followed by a surge, a gigantic whooshing, like some kind of monster machine had been activated.

Her left front tire dropped as though the Blazer had stumbled. Ginger looked to the right, toward the mountains, and saw some dark, colorless mass surging towards her.

The Blazer was slammed by a huge curtain of water and Ginger collided with the passenger door. The door flew off and she tumbled left, out of the car, off the bridge, and was swept along by the furious tide. No matter what was in its way, Ginger Kincaid included, this force was going to keep surging and shoving and nothing in the town of Lynton could stop it.

CHAPTER 42

The last thing Wolfpaw could remember was stretching out on the riverbank. Sometime during the night he'd stirred, sensing a hostile presence, then felt a tremendous concussion, as though he'd fallen from a great height, followed by overwhelming darkness.

But a light appeared in the distance, as though someone were holding a candle, and he moved toward it. He'd felt part of the darkness before, as though he'd melted into it, then slowly, drifting forward, his presence took on more and more dimension. He was walking, in a way, but the only thing he could compare it to were the few times he'd been in airports, swept along by those moving tracks that could carry you or you could move forward with the motion swiftly and with very little effort.

His surroundings came into a kind of misty focus and he realized he was still in Lynton. He could go anywhere at will and he floated to the mountains, communicating, not with humans but with creatures, letting them know what was going on with the town and who was responsible for spoiling things.

Wolfpaw was on Highway 38 now, the two-lane that continued east all the way through Kansas and beyond. He was on the shoulder, but it didn't really matter, he could have walked on the center line and wouldn't have been harmed and no one would even see him, because, by now Wolfpaw fully realized he was dead.

Someone had struck him with a hard object or maybe shot him as he slept. It probably had been those kids who hung around the bridge, the ones who'd attacked that Wendt fellow from Mentex, only to be chased off by the lion.

Wolfpaw was sorry to have had to interrupt who he was and what he was and didn't know what would be coming next. That was why he was making his way east and then north, back to where he'd been before setting off so many years ago.

That had been the second time he'd left home. The first had been when he'd joined the army. His father mocked him for it, but then his father had mocked him about nearly everything.

Wolfpaw was nineteen when he got to Vietnam. He hadn't seen much action. The unit he was in seemed to operate on its own, just setting out and poking around, occasionally trading fire with an all but invisible enemy. But there had been that one time. They came over a slight rise in some open terrain and encountered a platoon of VC who seemed as surprised as they were.

It was close fighting, not hand-to-hand, but tight and hot with M16s and small arms as well. Wolfpaw hadn't fired his rifle but watched the scene unfolding with detached fascination.

A few men went down; VC, as well as some of his own. Gerberding, a fresh-faced kid from New Jersey, took one in the head. He'd been about three yards away, close enough for Wolfpaw to have caught some of the boy's brains on his shoulder. He went down and Wolfpaw was amazed to see that seconds later, Gerberding's body, more like his body-within-a-body, was flailing around trying to pick up his rifle, only he couldn't get a grip on the stock or the barrel because that body, the one he had now, wasn't solid.

Wolfpaw had looked across the field and saw one VC rising like mist. He had another body forming above his fallen corpse and this one was like particles of light, getting more and more vivid. Wolfpaw, out of kind of a confounded fascination, fired a round that would have gone right through the heart but did nothing because there was no body, no heart.

Seeing what Wolfpaw attempted, the soldier-spirit grinned and performed a kind of dance, taunting him.

That was the only shot Wolfpaw fired and a minute later it was over.

He never told anyone what he experienced that day but it

gave him the knowledge that so-called death was merely an interruption.

A car was coming. Without thinking, Wolfpaw directed his motion into the highway, all the way to the center line. The car, small and shiny-new, screamed toward him at seventy, oblivious to his presence. The driver, just before the car reached Wolfpaw, swerved slightly away, as though sensing something in his path.

* * *

Todd and Cinda stood on a peak at dawn, looking down on the town. They'd managed to all but swim across Peach Orchard Road the night before, then kept moving higher until they were at a place where the water would not engulf them.

The town had been hit hard. They could see fierce, brown water rushing through it, the riverbanks overflowing, a furious tide shoving trees, rocks, appliances, anything in its wake. The river breaching would have been catastrophic enough. But Rabbit's Foot Rock had given way, an uncontrollable torrent gushing down the mountain from ten thousand feet above. At the far end of the devastation, the Mentex plant was completely engulfed in sludge and liquid. It looked to Todd as if anything that had been above ground – the bridge leading into the plant, the statue of Elias Howard Lynton, the glass-covered complex that housed Lowell Felker's office – were collapsed or sunk or submerged.

The warning they'd sounded likely saved some lives but with all the ruin they were seeing, there had to be hundreds who hadn't made it out. They knew they'd saved one life, Kent Kincaid, although he'd split off from them immediately, saying he was somehow going to make his way across town to find Ginger, the one part of his life that still meant anything.

"Look how the river's changed its course. It's branching out toward both sides of town."

"And look at the houses," said Cinda. "Some have been washed away and some are still standing. It's like the water was deciding which ones it would save."

"Looks like Ossie got off with a non-fatal hit," said Todd.

"I guess all those steps you have to walk up to get there came in handy," said Cinda.

"But how on earth are all those other people going to put their lives back together?"

Todd felt an unnamable wave of emotion rise up in him. "I think it's time to go back down and find out."

Taking hold of Cinda's hand, they slowly, carefully made their way along the steep slope, fully aware that the water had shifted things, making the very earth beneath them quite precarious.

They stopped.

"Did you hear that?" asked Todd.

"Sounds like an animal, but I can't tell what kind."

They stood frozen for a moment. Cinda pulled out her pistol.

Another sound, louder this time, infused with a distinctive high pitch.

Todd turned slowly.

Staring out at him from the mountain brush was a pair of eyes, glowing in the silver light. Todd felt a catch in his chest and throat as his breath stopped.

A dog, its reddish-brown coat covered with cockleburs and mud, pushed out into the open. It was big, with soft brown eyes and a welcoming expression.

Cinda laughed and put her gun back in its holster.

Todd crouched down, holding his arms out.

"Come here, my friend, come on over here."

The dog responded, seeming to wag its entire body as it weaved its way toward him.

Todd embraced it, and the two of them rolled to the ground, not caring about the mud; one laughing, the other whimpering with pleasure.

Cosmic Egg Books

FANTASY, SCI-FI, HORROR & PARANORMAL

If you prefer to spend your nights with Vampires and
Werewolves rather than the mundane then we publish the books
for you. If your preference is for Dragons and Faeries or Angels
and Demons – we should be your first stop. Perhaps your perfect
partner has artificial skin or comes from another planet – step
right this way. If your passion is Fantasy (including magical
realism and spiritual fantasy), Metaphysical Cosmology, Horror
or Science Fiction (including Steampunk), Cosmic Egg books
will feed your hunger. Our curiosity shop contains treasures you
will enjoy unearthing.
If you have enjoyed this book, why not tell other readers by
posting a review on your preferred book site. Recent bestsellers
from Cosmic Egg Books are:

The Zombie Rule Book
A Zombie Apocalypse Survival Guide
Tony Newton
The book the living-dead don't want you to have!
Paperback: 978-1-78279-334-2 ebook: 978-1-78279-333-5

Cryptogram
Because the Past is Never Past
Michael Tobert
Welcome to the dystopian world of 2050, where three lovers are haunted by echoes from eight-hundred years ago.
Paperback: 978-1-78279-681-7 ebook: 978-1-78279-680-0

Purefinder
Ben Gwalchmai
London, 1858. A child is dead; a man is blamed and dragged through hell in this Dantean tale of loss, mystery and fraternity.
Paperback: 978-1-78279-098-3 ebook: 978-1-78279-097-6

600ppm
A Novel of Climate Change
Clarke W. Owens
Nature is collapsing. The government doesn't want you to know why. Welcome to 2051 and 600ppm.
Paperback: 978-1-78279-992-4 ebook: 978-1-78279-993-1

Creations
William Mitchell
Earth 2040 is on the brink of disaster. Can Max Lowrie stop the self-replicating machines before it's too late?
Paperback: 978-1-78279-186-7 ebook: 978-1-78279-161-4

The Gawain Legacy
Jon Mackley
If you try to control every secret, secrets may end up controlling you.
Paperback: 978-1-78279-485-1 ebook: 978-1-78279-484-4

Mirror Image
Beth Murray

When Detective Jack Daniels discovers the journal of female serial killer Sarah he is dragged into a supernatural world, where people's dark sides are not always hidden.

Paperback: 978-1-78279-482-0 ebook: 978-1-78279-481-3

Moon Song
Elen Sentier

Tristan died too soon, Isoldé must bring him back to finish his job… to write the Moon Song.

Paperback: 978-1-78279-807-1 ebook: 978-1-78279-806-4

Perception
Alaric Albertsson

The first ship was sighted over St. Louis...and then St. Louis was gone.

Paperback: 978-1-78279-261-1 ebook: 978-1-78279-262-8

Readers of ebooks can buy or view any of these bestsellers by clicking on the live link in the title. Most titles are published in paperback and as an ebook. Paperbacks are available in traditional bookshops. Both print and ebook formats are available online.

Find more titles and sign up to our readers' newsletter at http://www.johnhuntpublishing.com/fiction
Follow us on Facebook at https://www.facebook.com/JHPfiction
and Twitter at https://twitter.com/JHPFiction